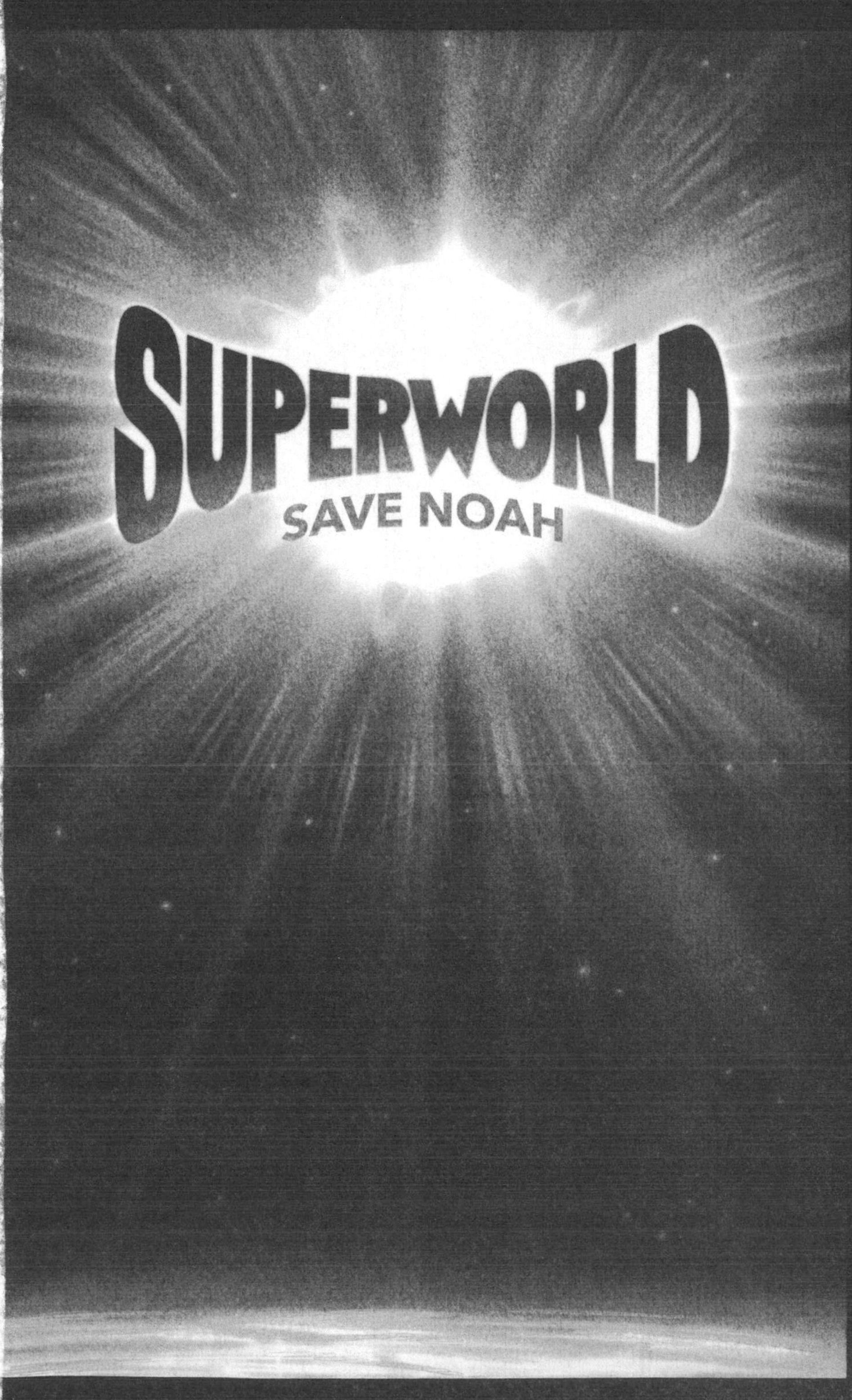
SUPERWORLD
SAVE NOAH

SUPER
SAVE

RANDOM HOUSE 🏠 NEW YORK

WORLD

NOAH

YARROW & CARRIE CHENEY

All rights reserved. Published in the United States by
Random House Children's Books,
a division of Penguin Random House LLC, New York.

Random House and the colophon are
registered trademarks of Penguin Random House LLC.

Visit us on the Web!
rhcbooks.com

Educators and librarians, for a variety of teaching tools, visit us at
RHTeachersLibrarians.com

Library of Congress Cataloging-in-Publication Data is available upon request.

ISBN 978-0-593-37537-2 (trade) — ISBN 978-0-593-37539-6 (lib. bdg.)
ISBN 978-0-593-37538-9 (ebook)

The artwork for this book was drawn and painted digitally.

Printed in the United States of America

10 9 8 7 6 5 4 3 2 1

First Edition

For our parents

CONTENTS

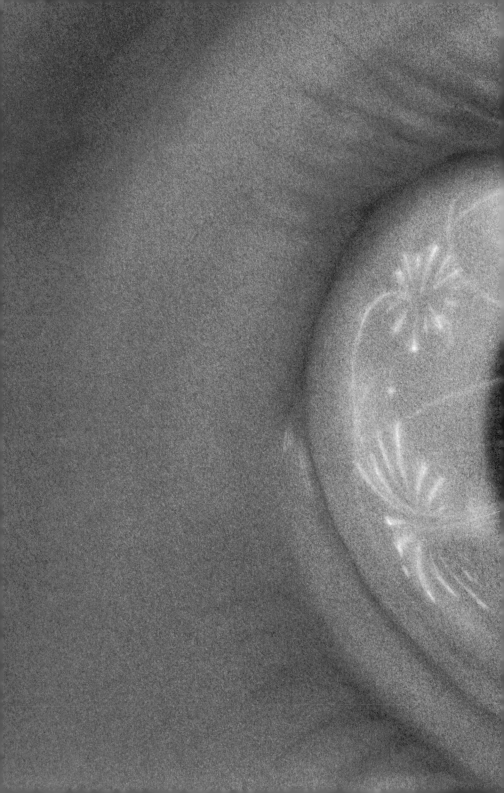

CHAPTER 1

Game On

I'm so sick of superheroes.

Okay, sorry. I'm just a little grumpy because I have eighteen broken bones right now. I think it's a personal record.

Hi, my name is **NOAH**, and I'm the only un-super person in **SUPERWORLD**.

I know what you're thinking: "Wait, you're the *only* pathetic weakling in a world full of super-people?"

Yup. I'm special that way. Special for being . . . un-special.

There is ONE thing I can do that nobody else can—I can *break*. So yeah, shattered bones and ruptured organs are business as usual for me. But today things *really* got out of hand.

Let's back up about thirty minutes. . . .

I was with my friends on this crazy-high cliff at the edge of town called Glacier Point. It's a nice spot, way above all the battles and nonsense. It's pretty safe up there, as long as you keep an eye out for the occasional stray energy beam or hurled car.

It's also the perfect launching point for a game my friends invented called SAVE NOAH—a surprise obstacle course designed to put me in *mortal danger,* over and over again.

One thing you've gotta understand about super-people—they're all sick with what I call "super-brain." It makes them obsessed with super stuff. They spend all day, every day, looking for excuses to switch into tights and capes. And unfortunately, I'm the world's only "innocent civilian," which means I'm the only dude super-people can actually *save.*

My friends are just as affected by super-brain as everyone else, so playing Save Noah helps get their super-wiggles out.

"Goonies."

On the bright side, we have an agreement. Every time I let them save me, they owe me pizza and a pre-Superworld movie—*NO SUPERHERO MOVIES ALLOWED.*

All right . . . game ON.

My friends backflip off the cliff and drop out of sight. Show-offs.

I back up twenty feet, tighten my shoelaces, zip up my vest, and take a deep breath.

I sprint toward the edge . . . and LEAP!

The first few seconds of free fall are amazing. I feel like I'm flying. I feel . . . *super,* like everyone else.

But the feeling doesn't last, 'cause I'm seconds from a supersonic belly-flop onto the jagged rocks below!

So now you're thinking: "Of course you broke eighteen bones, dummy, you just dove off a cliff!"

I get it, this looks bad. Mom would ground me for life if she saw me right now. But the thing is, this is actually the safest part of my day because my friends are *really* good at saving me.

Let me introduce you. . . .

First up is **ARTURO**.

His super-name is **REPLAY**.

He was a prodigy pro-level gamer before Superworld. Now, gaming *is* his superpower. Anything he can do in a video game, he can do in real life! His reflexes border on Spidey-style precognition.

He's got that "I'm a gamer, so I don't take anything seriously" thing going. He laughs a lot. Mostly at me. Especially when I look like a sidewalk pancake. He can be a punk, but he's saved my life more times than I can count, and he's always got my back.

FIRST-PERSON SHOOTER MODE

RPG MODE

MARIO KART MODE

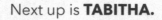

Next up is **TABITHA.**

Her super-name is **HAIRSTRIKE.**

Her super-hair is a picture of what's going on inside her head—ten things at once. Her mind never stops!

Her lightning-fast thinking makes her both the ultimate study buddy and the ultimate battle buddy. She can easily fight six villains while licking an ice cream cone and petting a puppy.

13

Here's my buddy **HUGH.**

His super-name is **HUGH-MONGOUS.**

Hugh is small for our age, so he gets picked on a lot. Which he *loves*. He's always looking for an excuse to GO BIG and return the favor!

And, pro tip: Make sure nothing valuable is lying around when he does. I'm pretty sure that skateboard is his dad's car.

Last, but definitely not least, is **IVY.**

Her super-name is **NIGHTINGALE.**

Ivy was my first friend when we moved here. We know pretty much everything about each other. Like I know she'd rather have no Slurpee than a cola-flavored Slurpee.

She's a little quieter than the rest of us. You know, the kind of person who talks less but thinks more.

Ivy notices *everything*— sounds, smells, how people are feeling. I don't mean that's her superpower. It's just kind of who she is.

But she *is* powerful. She's what's called a Fixer. Ivy can fix anything from a broken bridge to my broken bones!

Speaking of broken bones . . . I still have ZERO at this point in our game. Like I said, my friends are experts at saving me, which means being strapped to one of Arturo's home-brew death rockets is like playing in safe mode.

So what happened?

Well, see that dude in the Speedo, riding the subway train into that cliff over there? He just spotted me *"in peril."* Now every neuron in his super-brain lights up with one thought:

MUST SAVE SUPERWORLD'S
ONLY INNOCENT CIVILIAN!

I shout, "Game over, guys!" just as Speedo beelines toward me!

"*Pfff,* no problem," you say. "Your super-friends can take that guy, easy." Right, they can take *that* guy, but FIVE MORE HEROES just spotted Speedo rushing to my "rescue," which sent a burst of mental absurdity coursing through their super-brains!

Then TEN MORE heroes saw *those* heroes. . . . Then TWENTY MORE saw *those*. . . . Then THIRTY MORE . . .

My friends switch to evasive-maneuver mode. It's time to play keep-away!

Hugh-Mongous chucks me over a canyon to Nightingale. She fake-out tosses me under a burning bridge to Hairstrike.

Hairstrike lassos a gaggle of heroes and flings me through a half-collapsed building to Replay. Nightingale patches the building, cutting off a herd of heroes . . . who then CRASH through the fresh windowpanes!

The hero horde forces us deeper into the city, collecting heroes as we go, like a thousand cats chasing a laser-pointer dot. *And I'm the dot!*

Whoa, getting dizzy. . . . Can't see straight. . . . I'm all kinds of nauseous. So far, my friends are in control, always a half step ahead of the heroes. But this ain't our first rodeo, so we know what comes next. . . .

VILLAINS!

All across the city, villains see the hero storm cloud rushing overhead. Then, like a lightning bolt leaping from villain brain to villain brain, they're consumed by three simple words:

MUST. DEFEAT. HEROES.

THAT is when things get crazy . . .

. . . and bones get broken.

Which brings us back to where we started.

I feel like I'm in a swirly, painful dream as some rando hero peels me off the shattered concrete to take credit for "saving" me.

Aww, look how happy he is. I totally made his day. Sure, I'm in unimaginable pain, but isn't that a small price to pay for the smile on his pretty hero face?

NO. NO. NO TIMES INFINITY.

Okay, enough grumbling. The truth is, being mangled has a silver lining—it means Ivy has to heal me, which is pretty cool. It almost makes the terror, pain, nausea, and humiliation worth it. Almost.

I feel my bones mending and my heart rate stabilizing. The ringing in my ears fades as I hear *CLICK, CLICK, CLICK*. I see flashes as microphones whack my head and crowd my face.

I'm surrounded by reporters and news cameras. Oh look, I made the news. *Again.*

Ivy and I lock eyes. "Crud. The news!"

Everything up till now has been child's play. This day is about to get *way* more dangerous!

We hear the digitized squeal of wheels, then yelps from the crowd. A Tron Light Cycle skids to a stop in front of us, knocking reporters down like bowling pins.

It's Replay. "Hop on if you wanna live, bro!"

CHAPTER 2

The Home Game

Seconds later, I'm zooming home on top of Replay's Light Cycle.

"*Buuuuuusted!*" says Arturo, still in Replay mode. "You're gonna be *buuuuuusted*!" He's enjoying this way too much.

"Not if I get there first!"

If I don't get home before my parents, I'm dead. Okay, not actually dead. Worse. I can handle the temporary physical pain of broken bones. But being grounded is lasting pain. It means loss of freedom, something Ivy can't fix.

I check my watch—5:58 p.m.! TWO MINUTES UNTIL THE EVENING NEWS!

Arturo takes a hard ninety-degree corner. I struggle to keep my grip. "Couldn't you have picked something more passenger friendly?"

"Sure! Next time I'll drive you home on a Tetris block."

We streak down my street. Arturo slams on the brakes, catapulting me onto the front lawn.

I see the glow from the TV screen through our front window! Uh-oh.

"You want me to take care of that?" Arturo levels a plasma cannon at the window.

"NO! Not helpful!" I bolt for the front porch.

Arturo shrugs and the cannon dematerializes. He glides away on a Tetris block. "See ya *never. Buuuuuusted!*"

I rush through the front door—*SPLAT!* I'm lassoed by an enormous tentacle. It's a GIANT OCTOPUS with a GRANDMA HEAD!

Ugh, I should've seen this coming. Maybe your grandmother bakes or scrapbooks or whatever. Mine shape-shifts. Grandma can change into any creature, real or imagined. Her super-name is **GRANIMAL.**

Grandma's nasty suction cups smush over my mouth and nose. It tastes like seaweed mixed with boogers. Thanks, Grandma.

"You let your guard down, little man. *BIIIIG* mistake!"

Grandma's love language is personal assault. She loves to surprise attack me to hone my survival skills, which is why Mom won't let her live with us. We moved her down the block to the Old Oaks Home. FYI, that place is a death trap. Give a bunch of elderly people superpowers and immortality and, well, you do the math.

Granimal pins me to the ceiling. "Your move, pumpkin."

I shout, "Put me down!" but it sounds like "Mmffpff hmmmpfffmm!"

"How ya gonna survive in the real world if you can't throw down with a little old lady?"

Wait . . . my parents usually subdue Grandma within seconds of an attack. I must've beaten them home!

"What's the matter, honey? Is a scary octopus picking on you? Aww, Grandma will make it all better. How 'bout a little hug?"

Her tentacles twist around me . . . squeezing . . . constricting. . . . Blood rushes to my head.

I strain my bulging eyes to see the TV in the living room. My little sister, **JOY,** is watching a villain cartoon. So far, so good—no parents AND no news!

"Joy! HELP!" is what I try to squeeze from my lungs. But it comes out as a squeaky burp.

She totally hears me; she just doesn't care. If Joy felt like it, she could save me in two seconds. She's only six years old, but she's technically the most powerful person in the world.

Yeah, you heard that right.

Everyone else in Superworld has ONE dominant superpower, or Prime Power.

They have generic powers too—tons of people can fly, and everyone can be thrown through walls without getting a scratch. But their Prime Power is the one that defines them. Joy has two. TWO!

The day the meteorite hit, she got a double dose.

Wait, I haven't told you about the meteorite. Let's rewind again. This time we need to flash back FIVE YEARS to the day everything changed. . . .

You know how in comic books and superhero movies there's always an asteroid or magical crystal or radioactive whatever that gives some ordinary person superpowers? Yeah, that actually happened. Seriously. On my seventh birthday.

I'd planned the most epic birthday party ever. I picked a superhero theme because I was a mega-fan—the kind of kid who shoves a mattress out his second-floor window, suits up, and tries to fly. (First broken leg, BTW. Don't recommend.)

Dad and I spent three weeks making my awesome aluminum-foil Meteor Man costume. I had everybody come dressed as villains or reporters so I could be *THE* hero of the day.

There I was, the coolest guy at the party, ready to beat the candy guts out of the Thanos piñata, when a bright light streaked across the sky! Then . . .

BOOM! A meteorite slammed into Earth!

The ground shook, buildings cracked, trees toppled, cars rolled. . . . I watched in terror as my family and friends were swallowed up by waves of blinding, white-hot energy. Was this the end of the world?

Well, no. But also yes.

Suddenly everyone was flying, shooting lasers out of their eyeballs, and tossing cars like footballs! Lightning bolts came sizzling out of Dad's fingers, Mom stood forty feet tall, and my one-year-old sister was generating a tornado with her mind.

That was the moment superpowers were released into every person on Earth. Every person . . . but *me*.

"Why not you, Noah?" you ask. "What the heck?!"
Yeah, what the heck indeed!

Apparently I was the only human entirely covered in *aluminum foil* that day. That's right, my "awesome" costume shielded me from the superpower blast and deflected the power onto my baby sister. Talk about adding insult to injury!

Our parents gave Joy the super-name **PSYCHLONE** because her dual powers are telekinesis (which is a fancy way of saying she can move, throw, and crush things with her mind) and weather manipulation (which means taking the last cookie can result in a lightning strike). That name totally suits her—you can see a storm raging behind her freaky little eyes. I mean, look at her. She's creepy, right?

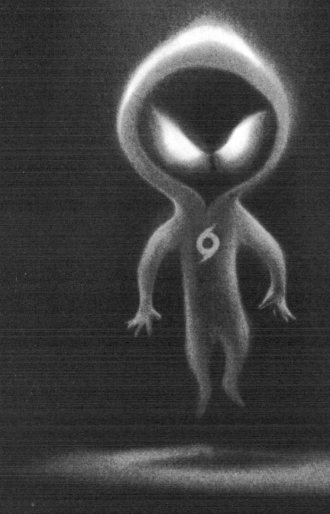

Mom and Dad think Joy will grow up to be a hero, but I'm worried. She has the potential to be the world's most powerful superhero, or our most powerful super-*villain*. I try to keep an eye on her. I may not be super, but I'm her big brother, so it's my job to protect her. Too bad she doesn't feel the same about me, 'cause Grandma is wiping the floor with me right now. Literally.

"Come on, dumpling, you're not even trying." Grandma's remaining tentacles start spinning like helicopter blades. What is she doing?!

"No more nice Granny!" Her whirling tendrils attack my head like a car wash. *Slap-slap-slap-slap-slap.* "Ouch-ouch-ouch-ouch . . ."

I'm about three seconds from blacking out when I hear the front door open and groceries hit the floor. "MOM! Put him down!"

It's my parents, **HIGH-RISE** and **SHOCKWAVE.** Mom super-sizes and rushes Grandma!

Lightning bolts stream out of Dad's fingers, electrifying Granimal. Unfortunately, this makes her tentacles involuntarily tighten! I'm like a twisted sheet of bubble wrap about to pop in a hundred places.

Thankfully, Granimal is stunned long enough for Mom to yank me from the slimy tentacles.

I smack the floor like a wet fish. I cough up a bunch of sea snot as my eyes focus and I see MYSELF on the TV! Joy is watching the news, that little traitor!

I check my parents. They're busy giving Grandma the third degree. They haven't noticed my bruised face plastered across the screen.

I whisper-yell to Joy, "Change the channel!"

She smirks and turns up the volume.

Grandma spots me on the TV. Our eyes lock, then she gives me an "Attaboy" nod and forms a thumbs-up with the tip of a tentacle. Unlike my parents, she always thinks it's cool when I make the news.

Joy cranks the volume so high you can hear it across the street. But before my parents look—*slap-slap-slap-slap*—Granimal assaults them with her helicopter tentacles! Yay, Grandma!

I leap for the remote, but Joy freezes me in midair with her brain.

"Come on, Joy, I can't get grounded again. *PLEEEEASE!*"

She pauses the TV on a full-screen shot of me broken on the sidewalk.

Lightning flashes in the entryway and I hear wet body blows. Granimal's diversion won't last much longer.

Think, Noah, think! How do you negotiate with a six-year-old who doesn't care about anything except . . . Wait, that's it!

"Joy, isn't it Dr. Destructo Week on the Villain Channel?"

She drops me like a slimy potato and changes the channel. Victory!

Joy LOOOOVES villains. They're pretty much all she cares about, and **DR. DESTRUCTO** is her favorite. His Prime Power is super-genius, so he's a master of deception, manipulation, and misdirection. He's also a super-genius *marketer*—every six months he launches an updated toy line, video game, cookbook, and chart-topping pop song to coincide with his latest upsized mech-suit. The guy literally gets BIGGER all the time. Currently, he's eighteen feet, four inches tall.

"Gee, Noah" is what you're thinking. "You sure know a lot about Dr. Why-Should-You-Care-O."

Yeah, tell me about it. That's because my obsessive sister babbles about him nonstop. Pretty much the only thing I don't know about Destructo is who he was *before* Superworld. Nobody knows his secret identity. Not even Joy. Apparently that just makes him cooler and more mysterious.

Destructo has been at the top of the villain charts four years running. Joy couldn't be happier—which for her means a really, really, *really* small grin.

45

A notebook floats into the room and hovers in front of Joy. It's stuffed with clippings, sticky notes, and papers. She flips it open with her mind power, then furiously jots down facts and stats from the Destructo documentary playing on TV.

Joy is way smart for her age. I don't think it's because of the meteorite; I think it's just how she's wired. When I was six, I was still struggling with my ABCs. But not her. It's like watching a miniature mad scientist at work.

I've gotta say, I'm curious to see inside her notebook, but I've never managed to get a good look because she guards it like it's her diary.

See what I mean? Creepy.

I pick my wobbly self up off the floor, then flick away as much Grandma goo as possible. I'm hecka disgusting, but at least I'm in one piece. Compared to the last five minutes, the rest of the night should be easy. I just have to keep my parents away from ALL news outlets until bedtime. No problem; I've become an expert at parental misdirection.

Grandma did a great job of stalling our dinner, so that helped. Then I stretched the meal out by thirty minutes by telling Mom about my really "dull" and "safe" day. Mom is a total worrier. She can shrink as well as grow, so she used to hide in my backpack to keep an eye on me at school. So embarrassing. But I kind of get it. It's gotta be hard having the only mortal kid in the world.

Next, I pepper Dad with questions about heroism. He's what you'd call an old-school hero. A golden-age-comics kind of guy—always speechifying about virtue, heroism, self-sacrifice, blah, blah, blah. Score, another hour down!

For the final stretch, I suggested we play Hero-opoly. Mom and Dad LOVED the idea. Parents are total suckers for kids who want to spend time with them.

And actually, family time can be pretty great for me too, because sometimes it triggers the old Mom and Dad—the ones who invented things like Friday Family Fun Night, First Floor Nerf War, and Couch Cushion Castle Clash.

I'm not a total villain for faking them out all evening just to save my hide. Mom and Dad laughed a ton, and Joy dominated Hero-opoly (though I suspect foul play). And for a little while, I didn't feel so different from the rest of my family.

Before I knew it, the news had come and gone, and my parents were grossing us out by kissing and cuddling while they did the dishes, causing Joy and me to retreat upstairs to bed.

Mission accomplished. I did it! I survived another twenty-four hours in Superworld.

This is my favorite part of the day. My heart can rest. I can breathe again. My mind can wander. I think about good things. About the world before—about *my* world.

But the moment never lasts long. Maybe ten or twenty seconds before I think about tomorrow. When it all begins again—in *their* world.

I really try to take things one day at a time. But it's hard not to worry when every morning I wake up the same, while the rest of them wake up even more powerful than the day before. What will this mean for me? And how many more super-battles can the world take? Am I the only person who realizes we're spinning through space on a giant ticking time bomb?

If I had power like everyone else, maybe I could do something to stop this craziness. Maybe I could save the good things in the world before they're all destroyed.

But I don't have what they have. So, what can I do?

Oh well, I'll think about it tomorrow. Right now, these recently healed bones need a good night's sleep.

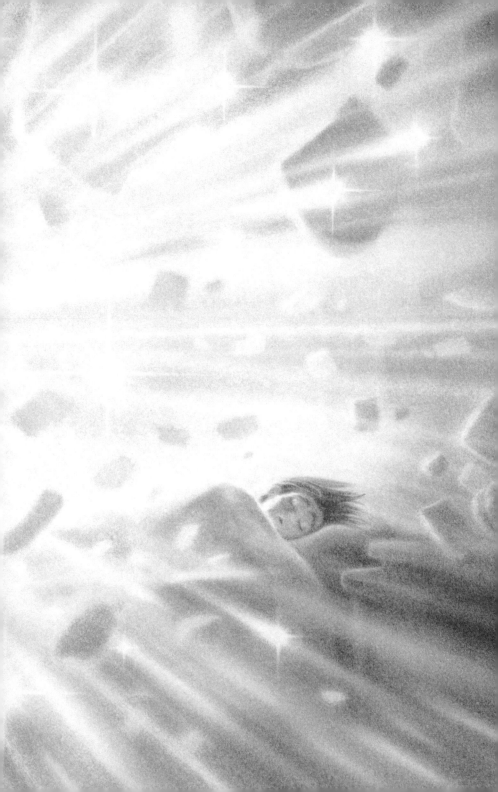

Man, I'm so sick of superheroes.

CHAPTER 3

Super-Spam

Ugh! SO frustrating! My eyes are on fire. I'm dead tired, but sleep is a no-go.

I glance through my nonexistent wall for a status check on the battle. Seriously? They're *JUST START-ING* the obligatory twenty-minutes-of-beating-on-each-other-with-zero-progress phase? It's 1:24 a.m.! They were supposed to stop at midnight.

We have a rule called the Power Pause where all fighting stops overnight so the Fixers can repair the city. Since everybody loves waking up to a fresh canvas, they used to obey the rule. But lately the battles are running longer and later. The Fixers can't keep up with the work, so every morning we wake up to a world more broken than the day before.

I grab my pillow and squeeze into my closet, shoving aside stacks of overdue library books. Don't worry, nobody cares about them anymore. I've actually been rescuing the books from the school library one armload at a time.

The muffled war zone fades away as I drift into a dream. I've had this one before. Lots of times, actually. I'm maybe three or four years old, watching a sunset with my parents. I feel safe. Or happy. Or more than that—like I belong.

Suddenly the sunset flashes, and the sky fills with fire! It's blinding, like the day the meteorite hit. Then—

BZZZZZZZZ!

I'm startled awake by a message on my phone!

"Press *9 to save the world."

Super-spam? Are you kidding me? It's not even 6 a.m.!

The rest of my morning is a barrage of the same—messages in my cereal box, on my watch, on my tablet, on the TV. . . .

Our SURVIVAL depends on YOU. Reply OK to save us all!

Become the HERO you were meant to be!

OK

Press **HERE** to save the world!

The world needs a hero!
PICK ME!

YES!

W is the TIME To fulfill your DESTINY!

SUPERWORLD NEEDS YOU!

TELL ME MORE

TODAY!!

ONLY YOU have the power to save
DESTRUCTION!
PERWORLD'S
SWER THE

THE W
YO

YOUR DESTINY AWAITS

AWESOME, LET'S GO!

ONLY YOU
Can save us all!

OK

SAVE SUPERWORLD!
SERIOUSLY, just hit the button.

THIS BUTTON RIGHT HERE!

V LIFE STARTS NOW!
have the power to save
LD from utter DESTRUCTI
E TIME to be SUPERWORL
HERO! WILL YOU ANSWER THE

I ignore the super-nonsense and focus on my actual mission: Slip out before Mom can take me to school.

ere meant to be!

Sure, it's *physically* safer if she does, but it's *socially* disastrous because Mom hovers. Like, literally; she'll make herself fifty feet tall, lean over my school, and ask everyone to be gentle with her "special boy."

Yeah, that's NOT an option, so I've devised dozens of ways to escape the house undetected. Today I go with the old "'gotta go number two,' then slip out the bathroom window" routine. Works like a charm!

I sneak behind the hedge, then reach the sidewalk. That's when I feel *them*. EYES, lots of eyes, all trained on me. It's the same every day. The neighbors, the mail lady, the cable guy . . . all tracking my every move. I see glimpses of bright spandex and dangling capes beneath their "secret identity" clothing. They're all just itching for a chance to save me—the world's only nameless, helpless, *savable* bystander. I'll show you what I mean.

I step; *they* step. I stop; *they* stop. I go; *they* go. Stop. Go. Stop. Go. . . .

Messing with them is fun, but I've gotta be careful. One misstep could set off another city-wide chain reaction.

My next potential hazard is just ahead—the Old Oaks Home.

A dozen of Grandma's silver-haired pals are in full super-suit mode. Man, I miss the days when old people didn't wear Lycra. Wait, super-suit mode?! That can mean only one thing: *Something's about to go down.*

Wait a second, where's Grandma?

I instinctively leap backward as a giant Grandma-headed boa constrictor slams onto the sidewalk where I was just walking!

"*Pfff,* nice try, Grandma."

"Ssssweetie!" she hisses. "You got lucky!"

"Or maybe I've gotten too fast for you!" I head down the block toward the bus stop.

"Watch your back, ssssweet pea! Overconfidenccce'll kill you before I do."

65

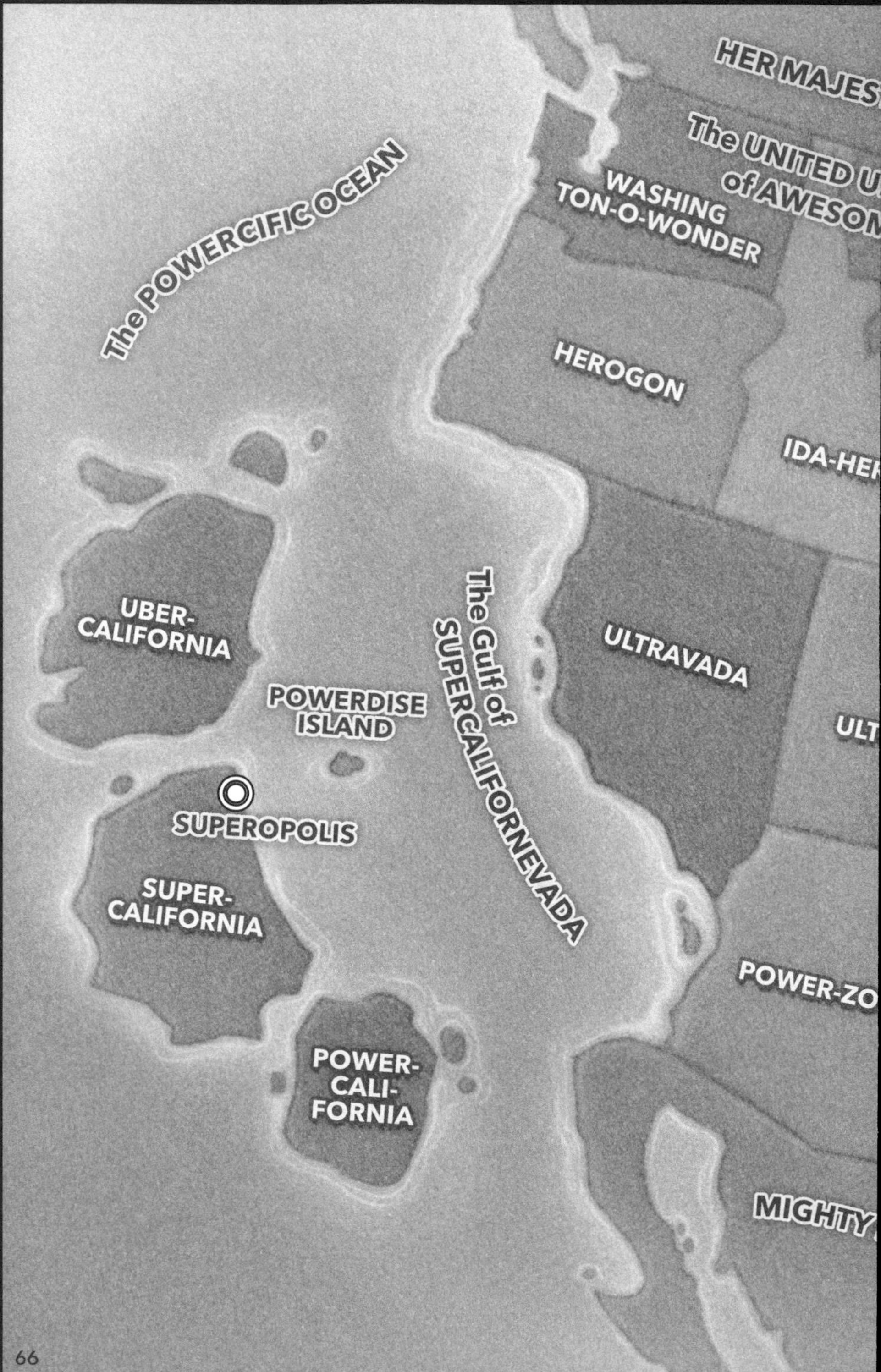

HER MAJES

The UNITED U
of AWESOM

The POWERCIFIC OCEAN

WASHING
TON-O-WONDER

HEROGON

IDA-HE

UBER-
CALIFORNIA

The Gulf of
SUPERCALIFORNEVADA

ULTRAVADA

POWERDISE
ISLAND

ULT

SUPEROPOLIS

SUPER-
CALIFORNIA

POWER-ZO

POWER-
CALI-
FORNIA

MIGHTY

66

The city bus skids to a stop at the corner. The driver cranks open the door. Everyone in the neighborhood piles on board, hoping to get a seat next to me, but I slip into an alley at the last second. I've learned to avoid every form of public transportation. Buses, subways, trolleys, and trains are death traps on wheels.

Remember Joy's favorite villain, Dr. Destructo? Well, about three months into Superworld, Blackjack and the Desert Defenders were hoping to hit number one on the hero charts by stopping him from turning Las Vegas into a Dr. Destructo theme park. It sparked a hero vs. villain dream battle known as the Californevada Conflict of Calamitous Awesomeness. Unfortunately, by the end of the day, California had cracked off into the Pacific Ocean.

That's where I live—on California. Well, the one in the middle, in what used to be Yosemite National Park. Now it's the coastal city of Superopolis.

N-A-POWER

UPER STATES
ERICA

EGA-TANA

WONDEROMING

RECTANGLE
OF
POWER

ULTRA
NEW
SUPER
MEXICO

THE
POWER STAR
SUPER STATE

MEXICO

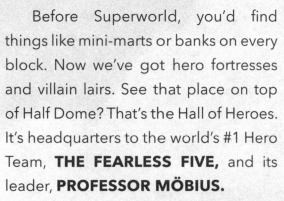

Before Superworld, you'd find things like mini-marts or banks on every block. Now we've got hero fortresses and villain lairs. See that place on top of Half Dome? That's the Hall of Heroes. It's headquarters to the world's #1 Hero Team, **THE FEARLESS FIVE,** and its leader, **PROFESSOR MÖBIUS.**

That's actually why we moved here. Mom figures Superopolis is the safest place for me in Superworld. Ha! As if more heroes equals more safety.

My route through the city is second nature to me, almost like a dance. I know when to walk, run, duck, and jump. But today, weird messages are throwing me off my game.

Just ahead, the crosswalk signal changes from DON'T WALK to SAVE WORLD. Huh? As I stare at it, a flaming runaway taxi careens right toward me!

Half-dressed superheroes rush to my aid, but I leap backward, dodging the cab on my own. Whoa, that was too close.

I keep my head down and hustle for the next few blocks. I'm back in the zone until I pass a flashing digital billboard that reads: THE WORLD NEEDS YOU, NOAH!

Wow. How do they personalize ads like that? Well, I suppose there could be lots of Noahs in Superopolis—

SIZZZZZZLE! Yikes! I dive into a dumpster. I'm only slightly singed by a fire-breathing land shark.

That's it, I am officially out of sync with my morning routine. I've gotta focus. I need to . . . Wow, it seriously reeks in here. I'm gonna need another shower—

CRUNCH! A giant crab claw grabs the dumpster and flings it, along with me, at a mob of villains swarming the carpool lane on an overpass. Oh great, I'm headed straight toward rush-hour battle traffic. I hope this doesn't make me late for school. Or dead.

Think, think, think. . . . Maybe I can dive out of the dumpster to safety before— Hey, is that me on that billboard over there?

CRUNCH-BOIIINGGG! The dumpster bounces off a giant rolling blowfish, ejecting me along with the rest of the garbage! I soar high over the Mighty Mini Mighty Mall. Yup, I'm definitely gonna be late, but at least the air up here is fresh. . . .

Who cares! Concentrate, Noah! How do you survive a crash landing? Stop, drop, and roll? NO, wait, that's for burning, *not* falling . . . *falling* . . . *FALLING!*

FLASH, a glowing sling thingy materializes beneath me, cradling me like a taco shell as it stretches down toward the ground.

Arturo is standing on the sidewalk in front of me!

"Thanks!" I say as I catch my breath. Dang, I stink.

"Playing Save Noah without us?" he says.

I shoot him my gimme-a-break look. "'Cause I'd ever do that, *ever.*"

"So how'd it go last night? Are you grounded for life?"

"Nope! I'm free as a flightless bird," I say.

"Man, you're good. Want a lift to school?"

"As long as it doesn't involve air travel."

"Prepare for takeoff." Arturo pulls his hand backward, causing the taco sling to do the same. Wait, I know what this thing is! It's a giant Angry Birds slingshot!

He lets go. *BING-WHIIIZZZZZZZZZZZ* . . .

Aaand I'm airborne again! Arcing over the city, heading straight for school. Well, at least I'll be on time. And alive. Probably.

CHAPTER 4

Getting Schooled

My flight path settles into a cheek-flapping nosedive!

SNAP-SNIP-SNAP! Hairy cords lasso my arms and legs as Tabitha sets me down at the entrance of our school, Half Dome Bay Hero Academy.

In Superworld, we have two types of schools—HERO schools and VILLAIN schools. Hero parents enroll their kids in hero schools; villain parents, in villain schools. But, no matter how much they want to believe it, villain parents don't always have villain kids, and hero parents don't always have hero kids. I'm pretty sure there are more villains in my school than people realize. And I'm definitely not convinced Joy should be at her hero elementary school.

Ivy and Hugh flank me on both sides. Hugh pinches his nose. "Man, you're smelly. And you guys say *I* should shower more."

Arturo swoops in next to Hugh. "Just because Noah smells like trash, it doesn't mean you should."

"Sorry for the stench," I say as I flick some rotten cottage cheese off my backpack. "I had a little trouble getting through the city."

Ivy scans me for damage. "Everything okay?"

"Yeah, thanks. I'm just a little off this morning. All good now, though. You guys ready?"

It used to be that surviving school meant surviving social dynamics, a scary teacher, pop quizzes, the cafeteria food, and death by boredom. That's all child's play compared to now.

My friends close ranks around me as we pass through the school entrance. This is strategic for two reasons— it provides protection and cloaking. The more I blend in, the better. Right now, if I could choose one power, it would definitely be invisibility!

My entourage shuffles me across the quad, then Ivy and I peel off and head to first period—Super Science.

Unfortunately, our science teacher believes in "experiential learning," so she's always inviting eager heroes to demonstrate the day's super-science-y subject.

Monday—The dos and don'ts of atom splitting.

Tuesday—Practical applications and dangers of ice powers.

Wednesday—Fun with the vacuum of space!

Today—We studied the thermodynamic properties of a heat beam as it collides with a classroom full of students. Ivy is currently replacing my hair and eyebrows.

When the bell rings, Ivy hands me off to Hugh for second period—Superworld History. He's pumped. "Dude, we're covering year one! It's totally my favorite!"

"Oh great. *Again.*"

"Except year two is *also* my favorite! Oh man, and year three was EPIC!"

Hugh loves this class, but I don't get it. I mean, I used to really like history. But now all we study is the last five years—since the meteorite hit—what our teacher calls "the only *important* history."

"Year four was good," Hugh says, "but I mean, it was only last year. Maybe I'm more of an old-school guy."

"Yeah, you're a real throwback." I put my head down to catch up on some z's. I slip into a dream. . . . I'm flying over our school. I can almost feel the wind on my face. . . .

No, wait, I *DO* feel the wind on my face! "Aaaaaagggghhhhh!"

That's because Hugh loves waking me up for third period by chucking me across the quad to Tabitha, who catches me with her hair!

As a result, I'm always wide awake for Mega Math. That's right, even math is super-themed.

MEGA MATH POWER QUIZ
Please show your work!

If Bombshell launches three Oblito-Rockets from a super-train traveling at 532 miles per hour, and the French Phantom fires his Baguette Bazooka while traveling in the opposite direction in his S-Car-GO at 323 kilometers per hour, who would win the battle before the train plunges off the crumbling bridge?

A. Bombshell

B. The French Phantom

C. The train isn't actually a train; it's the dastardly villain, Train-Wrecker, who turns the tables and defeats them both!

If our school is still in one piece by the end of math, Tabitha hands me to Arturo for the class I dread most. If you think PE used to be bad, imagine a game of flag football between the X-Men and the Justice League where the teams don't give a rat's behind about the innocent civilian (me) who just accidentally ended up with the ball. TERRIFYING. Even during Ping-Pong week, Ivy had to reattach my eyeball six times. Now Mom sends me with a note to get out of class. It's the one time I'm glad she's overprotective.

Coach blows his whistle. "Welcome to rugby week!"

No way, no how! I hand him my note and head across the football field.

Arturo shouts, "Try to survive forty-five minutes without me!"

As I pass beneath the scoreboard, it lights up with giant letters: ZERO OR HERO.

My phone buzzes with the same message. Enough with the spam! I turn off my phone.

Everyone's in class, so the campus is pretty safe. I hurry across the quad to my glorious refuge—the library. I'm the only person who goes there anymore.

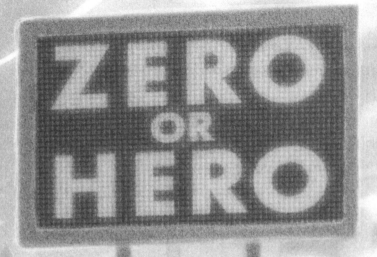

The bookshelves look like Swiss cheese. There are massive holes everywhere. I hear loud chomping coming from the History section. Oh man, he's at it again!

I hustle over piles of mutilated books until I reach the source of the noise—a ten-foot-long worm munching through the wonders of the ancient world.

I snatch the half-eaten book from **BOOKWORM's** enormous and disgusting mouth!

"Mr. Almaraz, we talked about this like a hundred times. You're a *librarian*! Don't you guys take some sort of oath to protect literature, art, history?"

His cheeks are stuffed with slobbery pages. "Nope, which technically means this is one hundred percent cool." He swallows a mouthful of history, then reaches for another snack.

I swipe it away. "It's not even one percent cool!"

Bookworm is getting hangry. "Noah, this isn't *your* library."

"I'm a student, so technically it is. Please, Mr. Almaraz, this stuff is important."

"Important?" He grabs another book. *"The Colosseum.* We don't need this. The Great Gladiaticus dropped it on Marcus Obliteratius last month." He gobbles up the cover.

"Give me that!" I shove the soggy book inside my backpack. "Can't you stick to the shelves and leave me the books?"

"Noah, I don't see why you're so obsessed with these relics. All this old stuff is passing away. We have *new* books. *Better* books! Have you read *The Invisible Hobbit*? Pure genius!"

"But I don't want the old stuff to be forgotten," I say. "Every book you eat is like watching myself being swallowed up."

"Whoa, Noah, that's deep. All right, all right. I hear you." He bites into a shelf instead.

Mr. Almaraz is a good guy, and I know there's a real librarian in there somewhere. He's just sick like everyone else. For the rest of the period, I do my best to work around his super-brain, quizzing him about the books he used to love. It takes a while, but he smiles as he remembers *Treasure Island, Frankenstein, The Odyssey,* Captain Underpants. . . . It gives me hope. Hope that maybe—

RIIINGGGGG! Oh no! The LUNCH BELL!

I shouldn't have turned off my phone! I have a daily alarm set for three minutes before the bell so I can get to my friends while it's still safe.

I dart for the exit, reminding Mr. Almaraz, "Remember, wood GOOD. Books BAD!"

I rush out the door but I'm too late. The quad is swarming with students. I feel waves of heat, cold, and static electricity as students reheat lunches, chill sodas, clash over the best spots on the lawn, and battle for the last slice of apple pie at the snack window. My friends are nowhere in sight.

I turn on my phone. Dozens of notifications slide across the screen. Mostly spam, but the last few are from my friends asking where I am.

I punch in "On my way!" and then take a deep breath. Okay, Noah, you can do this. I plunge into the swirling maze of deadly classmates. . . .

I keep my head down, no eye contact. Aaah! *Acid Girl!* I pop-vault and lemur-leap over the locker structure.

Fire Dude! I fake-out spin right, gecko-wall-run into the path of the *Battle Chess Club*!

I dive and shoulder-roll between the *Old-Schoolers* and the *Anti-Heroes*. I'm good. Fine. Just gotta focus.

I sidle up to the *Long Capes*, who shield me from the fight between the *Mega-Mathletes* and the *Robotics Cyborg Club*. Getting close now, looking for an opening . . .

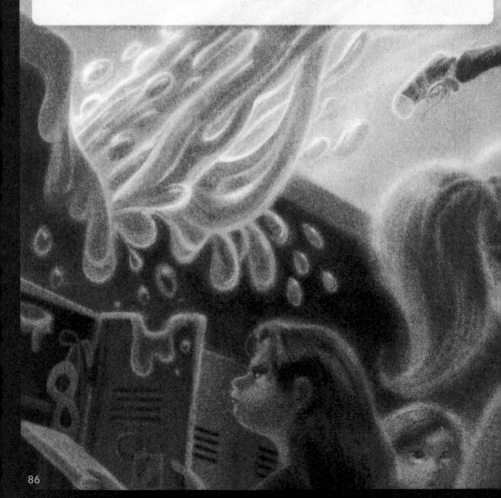

THERE! It's a straight shot to the end of the quad! I'm gonna make it!

WHAM! I'm slammed from behind. I stumble forward as EVERYTHING GOES BLACK.

CHAPTER 5

With Noah Power
Comes Noah Responsibility

I'm floating in infinite darkness. The only sound is my overclocked heartbeat, which probably means I'm not dead. So, yay for that.

How should I respond to this utter nothingness? First, I'll pretend I'm not a hundred percent terrified. Nope, total fail. I hate to admit it, but I could really use a superhero right about now.

Okay, I gotta do something. Let's go with yell. "HEEEEELP?! Is anybody out there?!"

Nothing.

Then a deafening movie-trailer voice thunders from the blackness: "SUPERWORLD IS IN GRAVE DANGER! . . . *DANGER . . . DANGER . . .*"

Wahoo, I'm *not* alone! "Hellooooo? Can you help–"

"WHO CAN SAVE IT? DOES *ANY* SUPERHERO HAVE THE POWER TO RESCUE THIS FRAGILE BLUE WATER BALLOON WE CALL HOME?"

Huh? Blue water balloon?!

"NO! NONE HAVE *THAT* POWER! . . . *POWER . . . POWER . . .*"

A bright, swirling cloud materializes in the blackness. It forms a giant, floating bald head sporting round sunglasses.

Hey, I know this guy, he's famous! It's Professor Möbius. What a relief! As #1 Hero Leader and genius mastermind, he's just the guy to help me.

"Excuse me, Professor Möbius? I think there's been a—"

"ARE WE TO BE RAVAGED BY DESPAIR? DOOMED TO OBLIVION?"

I guess he didn't hear me; I'll try again. "I'm sorry, Professor! I think you've got the wrong—"

"IS THERE NO ONE WHO CAN SAVE US?! YES! I MEAN, NO! THERE IS NOT NO ONE WHO CAN SAVE US."

What?

"THE ANSWER IS YES! THERE IS ONE! THOUGH NOT A SUPERHERO. NOT SUPER IN ANY WAY. A MERE MORTAL—"

Aaaand he's talking about *me*.

"NOT STRONG, BUT WEAK. NOT BRILLIANT, BUT AVERAGE. AWKWARD. UNATTRACTIVE. HARD TO GET AHOLD OF. YET *HE* IS OUR HOPE, FOR HIS POWERLESS-NESS IS HIS SUPERPOWER!"

Hard to get ahold of? Oh, I get it—the weird messages. Wait, *awkward*? *Unattractive*?

"NOAH, SUPERWORLD LOOKS TO YOU FOR ITS SALVATION!"

Salvation? *Me?* What's he talking about? Actually, he isn't talking. He's just staring at me, letting the moment sink in.

Still staring. Still . . . staring . . .

"Oh sorry," I say. "My turn? Umm, thanks, Professor. But you've got the wrong guy. I have a strict 'don't get involved' policy. May I go to lunch now?"

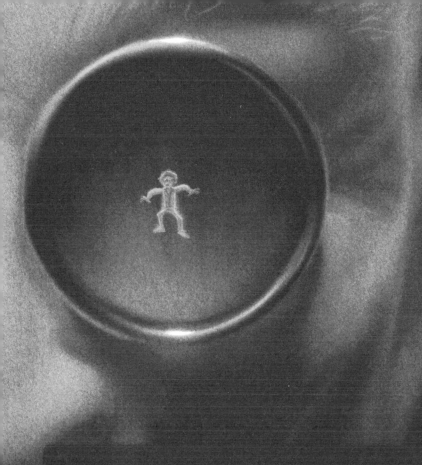

"LUNCH? *LUNCH?* I SPEAK OF PLANETARY OBLITERATION, AND YOU SPEAK OF TATER TOTS?"

"It's just that I skipped breakfast."

"NOAH, YOU *ARE* THE RIGHT GUY! YOU ARE THE *ONLY* GUY—THE ONLY ONE WHO CAN SAVE US FROM–"

"From what?" I say. "What can I possibly save anyone from?"

"FROM THE SUPER STONE!"

Okay, time out. I need to tell you about . . .

The Super Stone.

It's what they named the meteorite that gave everybody their superpowers. It's only the size of a softball, but it's the most powerful thing in Superworld—and the *most dangerous*. You know how the sun gives us life and energy, but you get too close and it's sizzle city? The Super Stone is like that. Step one millimeter inside its kill radius and *POOF!* You're history. Spontaneous combustion is the one thing heroes and villains are actually afraid of.

Möbius continues, "NOAH, THE SUPER STONE IS *LEAKING*, MAKING HEROES AND VILLAINS MORE POWERFUL EVERY DAY! YOU KNOW THE BATTLES HAVE GROWN MORE CATASTROPHIC. HOW LONG UNTIL EVERY VILLAIN POSSESSES THE POWER TO CRACK THE PLANET LIKE AN EGG, OR POP IT LIKE A WATER BALLOON?"

Okay, points for paying off the water-balloon thing. And he's totally right. It's nice to hear someone besides me is worried about this stuff.

His giant head leans in close. I cover my ears as he thunders, "THE SUPER STONE MUST BE CONTAINED BEFORE IT ANNIHILATES US ALL. AS THE ONLY POWER-LESS PERSON IN THE WORLD, YOU MIGHT BE IMMUNE TO ITS EFFECT. YOU MIGHT BE ABLE TO APPROACH AND SECURE IT WITHOUT DISINTEGRATING."

Okay, that's two "mights" too many. "Can't you just blast it or nuke it or something?"

"DESTROY IT? ABSURD! WITHOUT THE SUPER STONE, THE WORLD WOULD BECOME LIKE YOU AGAIN— PATHETIC AND POWERLESS."

"Really? Everything would go back to normal? That sounds awesome!"

"OF COURSE IT SOUNDS 'AWESOME' TO YOU! YOU HAVE NEVER TASTED SUPERNESS. YOU HAVE NEVER SAVORED SWEET, SWEET POWERFULNESS. YOUR MEDIOCRE TASTE BUDS LONG ONLY FOR THE FERMENTED, FISHY TASTE OF MEDIOCRITY."

"My taste buds long for fishy mediocrity?"

"PRECISELY! NOT TO MENTION, YOUR NAIVE IDEA IS IMPOSSIBLE. IT WOULD TAKE THE FUSION POWER OF A STAR TO DESTROY THE SUPER STONE. NO! WE CAN-NOT DESTROY IT, BUT WE CAN CONTAIN IT—SAVING THE WORLD FROM UTTER DESTRUCTION!"

Möbius leans so close I can feel the heat pulsing from his giant energy head. He speaks more softly, but it still rattles my rib cage.

"NOAH, I BELIEVE YOU ARE ON THIS PLANET FOR A REASON. YOU, AND YOU ALONE, CAN SAVE US ALL.

ARE YOU READY TO FULFILL YOUR DESTINY? ARE YOU READY TO BE . . . A *HERO*?"

Is this for real? Does the world really need *me*? Am I different for a reason? For a purpose? My heart is pounding, my mind spinning until—

I spot my tiny reflection in his dark spectacles. I'm framed by the rims of the giant granny glasses sitting on the disembodied hologram head of the insane leader of the world's most deluded super-team.

I can't believe I'm falling for this ridiculosity! Reality check, Noah—you've been kidnapped and taken to a sensory-deprivation alternate universe to be brainwashed!

I look Möbius straight in the glasses. "Am I ready to be a hero?"

He smiles. "YES."

"No."

He's perplexed. "I DON'T THINK YOU UNDERSTOOD MY QUESTION."

"No."

"NO, YOU UNDERSTOOD IT?"

"Yes."

"YES, YOU ARE READY TO BE A HERO?"

"No."

"PERHAPS I NEED TO USE SMALLER WORDS FOR YOUR SMALLER MIND."

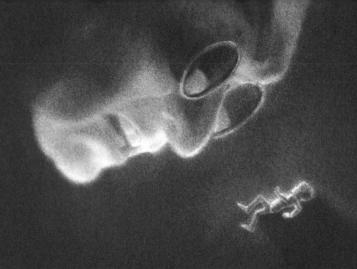

"No, I understand perfectly. It's just that I have zero interest in playing Save the World with you guys. Thanks, but you'll need to find some other sucker."

Möbius is baffled. "BUT THERE ARE NO OTHER SUCKERS . . . UHH . . . HEROES. DON'T YOU WANT TO SAVE THE WORLD?"

I shrug. "Meh."

Steam rises from his enormous head. "I SEE! SO, YOU ARE A *VILLAIN*!"

"Whoa, whoa, whoa. Simmer down. I'm *not* a villain. I just don't wanna play your hero game."

"THIS IS NOT A GAME!"

"Right, uh-huh. Sure, fine, whatever. Point is, I'm not your guy. Can I go?"

His expression turns cold. A harsh blue light illuminates his face from below like he's telling a ghost story with a flashlight under his chin, "IF YOU ARE NOT WITH US, YOU ARE AGAINST US. HENCEFORTH, YOU SHALL NO LONGER ENJOY THE BENEFITS OF HERO PROTECTION."

Okay, *now* I'm interested! Really! You're serious? From now on, half of the planet will leave me alone? Man, this whole kidnapping thing was totally worth it."

He smirks. "WE SHALL SEE, NOAH. WE SHALL SEE."

His head swirls, then vanishes. I'm alone again in the endless void.

"Umm, excuse me? Can I get a ride home?"

FLASH! I'm blinded!

I shield my eyes and feel a pair of goggles. I yank them off. My eyes focus and see . . . I'm still at school, standing in the middle of the crowded quad.

Phones buzz all around as every student gets a Hall of Heroes alert. My status just changed from "innocent civilian" to "VILLAIN"!

CHAPTER 6
No Villains Allowed

Our campus has a strict NO VILLAINS ALLOWED policy, which means I'm suddenly public school enemy number one!

All around me, students switch into super-suits, eyes blaze, powers sizzle and glow!

I raise my hands. "Wait, wait, wait, I'm *not* a villain. Let's talk about this. It's just a simple misunderstanding." Everything should be fine. Heroes can't attack me if I surrender, right?

THUD!

CATFIGHT

HIT-MAN

A super-sized "hero" named **AWESOMUS MAXIMUS** crashes down directly in front of me in that ridiculous pose on one knee and one fist.

"That's not our problem, *villain*!"

THUD, THUD, THUD! Three more "heroes" land all around me.

One thing the meteorite didn't change—every school still has its standard pack of thugs who think they run the place. Our particular litter of sick puppies call themselves

THE MAGNIFICENT MUSCLES.

Seriously.

AWESOMUS
MAXIMUS

BONE HEAD

I scan the crowd for my crew—not a friendly face in sight. That's okay. I've still got time because super-people always start with an opening speech.

Maximus gives each of his biceps a little kiss. "Locked and loaded. Any last words?"

That's his speech? It was, like, two seconds! Oh wait, he asked me a question. . . . Perfect!

"Ummm, any last words? Yeah, I just want to say that it's pretty cool you guys are, like, shellfish experts. Do you prefer steaming or sautéing? Personally, I love butter, so . . ."

Maximus is confused. He lowers his fists. "What? No, you loser. We're the Magnificent MUSCLES, not MUSSELS!"

"Yeah, yeah, I know. I love clam chowder, but I've never tried mussels. I hear some people are allergic and—"

BONE HEAD joins the convo. "Oh man, I'm totally allergic. One time I ate oysters and my tongue swelled up so big I almost choked on it."

HIT-MAN chimes in. "No way, me too! Not the jumbo-tongue thing, but I get nasty diarrhea and my face breaks out in these purple . . ."

While they bond over rashes, I text "911" to my friends. Crud! MESSAGE FAILED TO SEND.

Hero Wireless suspended my service.

Maximus slugs Hit-Man and Bone Head! "Focus, dummies! He's using villain trickery."

"DUCK!"

That sounds like Hugh. I hit the deck!

SMACK! Hugh-Mongous heel-kicks Maximus onto his gluteus!

Nightingale lands in front of me. "Noah, what's going on?!"

"Long story, but I'm *not* a villain!"

Replay and Hairstrike land behind Nightingale. Replay throws a Mega Man force field around me. "Sit tight, Noah. We'll exterminate these gym rats for ya!"

My friends are overconfident but awesome—always willing to be beaten to a pulp to keep me in one piece.

Maximus grins. "Anyone who *defends* a villain"—he looks around at the crowd—"*IS* A VILLAIN!"

Uh-oh.

The school mob descends upon my friends. Maximus drop-kicks Replay into the lockers. My force field vanishes!

SNAP! A tail whips around me! **CATFIGHT** sling-shots me into the air! "Aaaaaagh!"

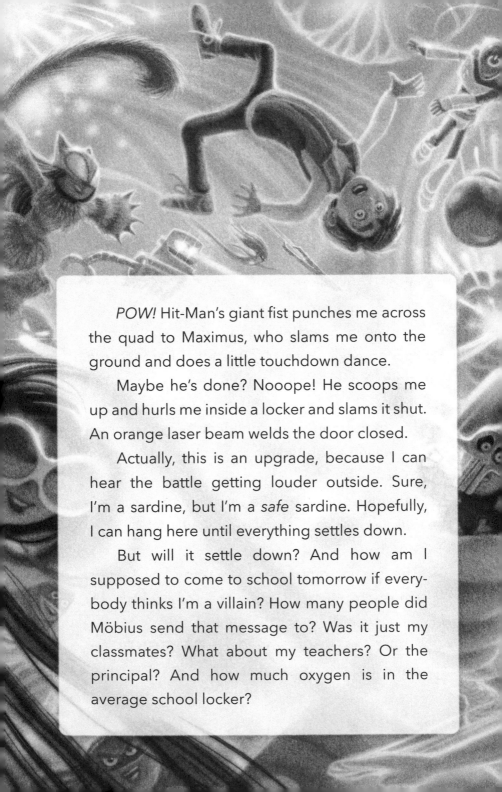

POW! Hit-Man's giant fist punches me across the quad to Maximus, who slams me onto the ground and does a little touchdown dance.

Maybe he's done? Nooope! He scoops me up and hurls me inside a locker and slams it shut. An orange laser beam welds the door closed.

Actually, this is an upgrade, because I can hear the battle getting louder outside. Sure, I'm a sardine, but I'm a *safe* sardine. Hopefully, I can hang here until everything settles down.

But will it settle down? And how am I supposed to come to school tomorrow if everybody thinks I'm a villain? How many people did Möbius send that message to? Was it just my classmates? What about my teachers? Or the principal? And how much oxygen is in the average school locker?

I hear screaming! The battle has taken a turn. I can't tell what's going on, but I hear lots of crashing and slamming. The locker rattles like we're having an earthquake.

Then I hear SNIFFING. Loud sniffing. It's getting closer. . . .

CRUNCH!

Gigantic teeth yank the locker door off its hinges. I'm face to face with Little Red Riding Hood's worst nightmare—a giant wolf with a pearl necklace and a fluffy blue hairdo!

"Hi, Grandma."

Behind her, the Old Oaks residents carpet-bomb my classmates with their old-school superpowers—*KAPOW! WHAM! BLAMMO!*

Grandma spits out the locker door, nailing Bone Head as he flees from Grandma's knitting partners.

"How's your day, sweet pea? Still feeling confident?"

"Grandma, how did you know . . . ?"

"Your little villain alert went city-wide."

City-wide? Oh no.

BOOM . . . BOOM . . . BOOM . . . BOOM . . .

Crud, that's not Godzilla we're hearing.

"NOAH?! Where's my baby?!"

The voice echoes through the school as a gargantuan Mom-shaped shadow fills the quad.

Granimal gives me a giant, toothy smile. "Sorry, sweetie, you're toast."

CHAPTER 7

Zero or Hero

"A villain?!"

"Mom, I promise I'm *not* a villain!"

She slaps a stack of paperwork on the kitchen table. She can't help growing when she's angry, so she's about seven feet tall right now.

"You're being transferred to a villain school! A *VILLAIN* school! Your friends won't be there to protect you. What if you get hurt? Ivy won't be there to . . ." Mom is furious, but also holding back tears.

Dad is quiet, his hair standing straight up. The room buzzes with static electricity. He gets this way when he's trying not to electrocute me.

Joy, on the other hand, is intrigued. A Sharpie and a fresh notebook float into her hands. She draws a picture of me on the cover.

Dad breaks his silence. "Noah, *what* happened? What did you *do*?"

"I didn't do anything. This isn't my fault!"

He shakes his head. "We didn't raise you to be dishonest. And we definitely didn't raise you to be a *villain*." Electrical arcs leap from his head to the sink and toaster. The fibers on my clothes stand on end.

"But I'm not lying. I have *ZERO* power, so how could I possibly be a villain? Or a hero for that matter? That's what you and Professor Möbius don't understand—"

"Professor Möbius?!" blurt Mom, Dad, and Joy in unison.

"Yeah, *Professor Möbius*! He kidnapped me and tried to force me to save the world. But since that's completely ludicrous, I told him no. So now he's mad and punishing me."

Dad sparks and sizzles all over. Burned toast ejects from the toaster!

Mom passes eight feet! "Let me get this straight. The world's greatest HERO leader KIDNAPPED you . . . because he wants *YOU* to save the world?!"

"I know. It sounds bananas, but let me explain—"

Mom's head hits the ceiling, which always means "This conversation is over! Go to your room, Noah! Expect to be there a long time!"

Whatever, I give up! This is so unfair. I do everything I can to *avoid* super-nonsense, and I still end up grounded!

I stomp up the stairs. My head feels like . . . I don't know . . . like it's about to pop. I want to escape to Glacier Point, but my bedroom will have to do. I've gotta clear my mind. I need to be alone.

"I have questions."

"Agghh!" My heart leaps into my throat.

Joy is floating in the hallway right behind me.

"Leave me alone, Joy. I mean it!" I slam my bedroom door in her spooky face and turn the lock.

The lock unclicks and the door swings open. Joy floats right inside like it's *her* room.

I want to shove her back out, but I know better. She'd just pin me to the wall or wrap my clothes around me like a straitjacket. My only option is a snarky comment: "Don't you have a doll to decapitate or something?"

She fakes a little laugh. "You're so funny." She opens her NOAH notebook to the first page. "Question number one: What's your villain name?"

"My what? This is so lame. I'm not a villain. *You're* a villain!"

She smiles. "That's exactly what a villain would say. Come on," she whispers, "you can tell me."

"Okay, fine. I'll spell it for you: *G . . . E . . . T . . .*"

Joy jots down the letters. "Uh-huh . . ."

"*O . . . U . . . T . . . Exclamation point.*"

She shoots me the stink eye.

"Listen, Joy. For the billionth time, I am not a villain. But you know what, I could've been a hero. Instead, *YOU* got *MY* power! *NOW* I'm . . . I'm just . . . *nothing*."

Joy lowers the notebook. "You aren't nothing."

"Yeah, whatever. Easy for you to say, little Miss Double Trouble."

I plop down on the edge of my bed and rub my forehead. I'm sweating; my hands are trembling.

"You don't need *power* to be a hero," she says with unblinking eyes. "Being a hero is a *choice*."

I roll my eyes. "Great, it's not enough that I had to suffer through a hero lecture from the world's #1 Hero Leader, now I have to hear one from the world's most powerful villain."

She perks up. "Dr. Destructo?"

"No, Joy. You! What do *you* know about being a hero?!"

Her face is cold as stone, then her lips twitch with a tiny smile she doesn't mean for me to see. She's so weird! Why do I let her get to me?

I close my eyes. "Would you please, please just go?"

I wait a few seconds . . . and open my eyes. Crud, she's still here.

"I have forty-nine more questions."

"Fine, I'll go!" I step inside my closet and pull the door shut.

I hold the knob and wait for the door to be yanked open. . . .

But it isn't.

I exhale, step back, and slide down the wall.

My hands are shaking. That figures. I don't even have control over my own body!

I have to calm down. I take a few deep breaths and try to quiet my mind. It's helping. The chaos in my brain and chest is starting to settle. . . .

My phone buzzes. It's Arturo:

**Dude, we're on hero suspension.
What's going on?!**

Hugh, Tabitha, and Ivy ping me too.
I feel sick to my stomach.

My friends are in trouble, my parents are furious, my little sister dominates me, every hero wants to fight me, I'm switching to a villain school . . . Oh, and the world's about to end, so nothing matters anyway.

I always thought that someday I'd figure it all out. That I'd end up *doing* something, or *being* something, I don't know . . . *special*. Not that I'd be super, just that someday I'd understand why I'm not.

Is there any chance Professor Möbius is right about me? Is this why I'm here? Or am I just falling for an idiotic super-charade because deep down, I want to believe I'm something rather than nothing?

My phone lights up the closet again. I squint to read the bright screen—it's Professor Möbius!

Second chance, Noah.
ZERO or HERO?

Wow, he's like a mind reader!

A glint in the corner of the closet catches my eye. The light from my phone is reflecting off some aluminum foil in a cardboard box. It's my old Meteor Man costume. I pull it out— it's crinkled and dusty, but the M logo on the chest is still good as new. I spent forever getting this just right. It was so important to me.

What would seven-year-old me have done if asked to save the world? No question, he'd have saved it by dinner time!

I feel something like butterflies in my chest. No, it's more like energy. I want to jump up and *DO* something! Maybe the seven-year-old me isn't completely gone.

But suddenly my mind floods with doubt—a thousand reasons why I should just hide in the dark forever.

Then my heart fights back! I feel a deep, steady power growing in my chest. . . .

I don't want to lose this feeling, and I know I will if I don't side with my heart right now.

I draw a deep breath. I type:

HERO

I hold the air in my lungs . . . theeeeeen . . . hiiiiit . . . *SEND!*

I did it! I exhale.

Okay, now what? I guess wait for a reply?

Nothing so far.

But I already feel better. My hands aren't shaking and—

Wait, yes, they are. Actually *everything* is shaking! My closet accelerates up, then forward! Faster, faster . . .

What's going on?!

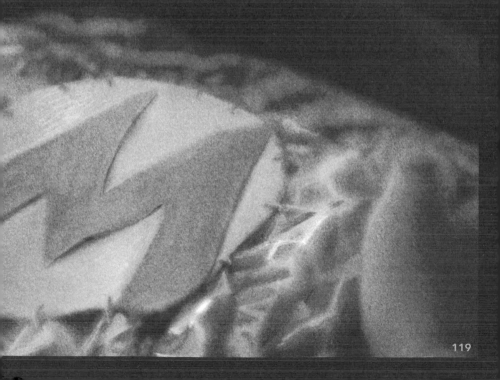

CHAPTER 8

The Super Stone

Sweaters, shoes, and library books bury me alive as the rising g-force pins me to the back of the closet.

Where am I going?! Maybe to the Super Stone? Cool, I can save the world and be back before my parents find out I'm gone.

I hope I get there soon because I can feel the blood rushing from my brain to the back of my skull . . . along with my face. I'm just seconds away from . . . black . . . ing . . . out.

SLAM! The closet stops, ejecting me along with the rest of its contents. I hit a cold stone floor and squeeeeeak to a halt.

"Oops-a-daisy, sorry for the bumpy landing!"

What? Huh? The blood rushes back into my brain, and my eyes begin to focus. I'm lying on the floor of a gigantic polished-marble room, if you can call a place like this a "room." I see lots of columns and superhero statues. A massive Hall of Heroes logo is floating at one end.

UNICORN MAGIC

A woman with a blue-and-gold super-suit and a unicorn head is standing over me. It's **UNICORN MAGIC,** one of the members of the Fearless Five! She waves her hoof-hand. "Up you go!" Magic sparkles lift me to my feet.

I'm embarrassed to say I'm a little starstruck. I'm also embarrassed that my personal belongings are scattered across the floor of the Hall of Heroes.

"BEHOLD! NEW HUMANITY'S ONLY HOPE! . . .
HOPE . . . HOPE . . ."

I know that echoey voice. I spin around and see
Professor Möbius's giant floating head above my
detached closet.

And that's not all—**MINDSTORM** is standing next to
him with an intense look on her face, like she's staring
into my soul. Which she probably is.

MINDSTORM

SPIDER MONKEY

And there's **SPIDER MONKEY**—who for some reason finds all of my personal items hilarious.

"*Noah* is our only hope?"

I know *that* voice too!

Everyone knows that voice. It's the world's most famous and idolized superhero—**MANTASTIC**! And no way, he knows my name? Okay, sorry, I'll recover my "I don't care" attitude soon. Right now, I'm having an involuntary fanboy moment.

"Seriously, *this* guy?" says Mantastic. "There's gotta be someone else. Anyone else."

Aaaand the moment's over.

THE FANTASTIC
MANTASTIC

Mantastic scans me up and down. "I mean, look at him. . . . He's awkward, weak, tiny. . . ."

"What's wrong with being tiny?!"

Aaah! *That* voice came from my shoulder! Whiskers tickle my cheek. It's the last member of the Five—**THE INVISIBLE RAT**—who's easy to forget for obvious reasons.

"Fine, Rat." Mantastic rolls his eyes. "He's wonderfully tiny. But he's still awkward and weak."

«I think he's cute.»

Aaah! *That* voice came from *inside my head*!

Unicorn Magic bubbles, "Mindstorm is right! If I had fingers, I'd squeeze Noah's little cheeks so hard they'd turn purple!"

THE INVISIBLE **RAT**

Mantastic interrupts. "Fight over your new boyfriend later. Right now we've got a world to save, and it's back to the drawing board. I say we give the trained monkeys another chance."

Trained monkeys? Not cool. "Look, if you guys don't need me, I'll just go home." I march toward my closet.

"STOP!" booms Möbius. "NOAH HAS SOME-THING MONKEYS DO NOT! NOAH HAS COURAGE! . . . *COURAGE . . . COURAGE . . .*"

Okay, that's more like it. And I think the fact that I'm here does prove that I have a little bit of—

Spider Monkey sighs. "Please, if you dangle a banana, monkeys have courage."

"INDEED, BUT NOAH ALSO HAS IMMUNITY! . . . *IMMUNITY . . . IMMUNITY . . .* NOAH IS IMMUNE TO THE DEADLY EFFECTS OF THE SUPER STONE! WELL, PROBABLY, HOPEFULLY."

Probably? Hopefully? Okay this is a terrible idea. "I'm with Mantastic. I vote for the monkeys."

"AND LASTLY, NOAH CAN MINDLESSLY FOLLOW INSTRUCTIONS—SOMETHING NO MONKEY CAN DO."

Spider Monkey nods. "True that."

"Right, I'm outta here." I step inside my closet and yank the door shut.

Okay, now what? They'll send me home, right?

Nothing's happening. Still nothing. Are they just standing there waiting for me to come back out? They've gotta realize this whole thing is a huge mistake. I mean, I'm not like them. I don't have super-powers.

«But you do have courage, Noah.» Mindstorm's voice fills my brain. «Not banana courage, REAL courage.»

Whoa, that's weird. How would she know?

«I sense it in you.»

Wait, did Mindstorm just read my thoughts? I think at her, «ARE YOU READING MY THOUGHTS?!»

«Sure am. It's my mind link. It's how we communicate during battles.»

«Whoa, this is freaky.»

«Freaky, but cool,» thinks Mindstorm. *«Listen, Noah, you're on our team now, so we've got your back.»*

«I don't think Jerktastic has my back.»

«What'd you call me?» thinks Mantastic.

«Wait, Mantastic is here too?»

Spider Monkey mind-laughs. *«Jerktastic. I'm totally using that!»*

«Geez!» I think. *«How many people are on this thing?!»*

«All of us,» says the Invisible Rat. *«Plus, I'm on your shoulder.»*

Aaagh! I leap out of the closet. "Stop doing that, Rat! Seriously!"

"THAT'S BETTER!" Möbius says with his actual, outside-of-my-head voice. "NOW, WHERE WERE WE?"

"Noah was handing out nicknames," says Mantastic, "but I suppose I deserved it. Peace, bro?" He extends his perfectly sculpted hand.

"Yeah, I guess." I shake it. Wow, that's a ridiculously firm handshake.

"Awww, you guys." Unicorn Magic sniffles with her horse nose. "So sweet."

"Stuff it, Magic." Mantastic releases his iron grip.

I massage the blood back into my hand. "Okay, so what's the plan? And how long will it take, because—"

"THE PLAN!" Möbius's voice echoes through the Hall of Heroes as the lights dim. "BEHOLD, MY LATEST INVENTION—THE SUPER STONE CONTROLLER."

A giant 3D hologram fills the room. It's a ring-shaped device with a dial covered in little icons.

A holographic Super Stone appears and flies into the controller.

SUPER STONE
CONTROLLER

131

"NOAH, YOU WILL PLACE THE SUPER STONE INSIDE THE CONTROLLER, STOP THE POWER LEAK, AND THUS . . . SAVE THE WORLD!"

Unicorn Magic fills the room with celebratory stardust!

"Okay, cool. So I pop the Stone inside that

SUPER STONE
SECURED = WORLD
SAVED!

controller thing, and we're good? Sounds easy."

Mantastic glares, "Easy? Saving the world is never easy."

"Okay, sure. Anyway, can we just do it now? I'm kind of grounded because of you guys, so I need to get home before—"

"Dude, are you serious?" says Mantastic.

Möbius shakes his giant head. "WHAT ARE THEY TEACHING IN HERO SCHOOLS THESE DAYS?"

He projects more holograms above our heads as Unicorn Magic explains a bunch of stuff I guess I should already know.

ONE DAY AFTER IMPACT

"Since its impact, the Super Stone has sat untouched in what used to be a vast desert. This location quickly became a pilgrimage site for fans worldwide.

ONE WEEK AFTER IMPACT

"Soon hotels, restaurants, and souvenir shops sprang up all around, leading to the creation of the most awesome super-theme park the world has ever known—Power Park!

ONE MONTH AFTER IMPACT

STONEYS SOUVENIRS

"Enclosing the Super Stone at the park's center is a heavily guarded and fortified structure called the Power Dome.

THE POWER DOME

THE SUPER STONE

"The Dome has two purposes:
1. It prevents the spontaneous combustion of over-enthusiastic tourists.
2. It prevents villains from stealing the Stone, then ruling the world with its unlimited power!

"Noah, this next part is *very important*—access to the Power Dome is permitted only during the crowning ceremony for a *NEW #1 Hero Team*."

Everyone looks at me.

"What? What did I miss?"

"NOAH," says Möbius, "YOU WILL GAIN ACCESS TO THE DOME AND SUPER STONE WHEN YOU BECOME THE LEADER OF THE WORLD'S NEW #1 HERO TEAM!"

I laugh, but he looks dead serious. "Wait, I thought you were joking."

"I DO NOT JOKE. I ASSUMED THIS WAS OBVIOUS. MANTASTIC HAS CAREFULLY SELECTED YOUR TEAM MEMBERS. TRAINING BEGINS TOMORROW."

"They're epic," says Mantastic. "You're gonna love 'em!"

What?! It took me years to figure out how to safely hang with my best friends. Now they want me to play superhero with a bunch of mini-Mantastics I've never met?

"Whoa, whoa, whoa," I say. "I have a better idea. If you need a super team, my friends would—"

Möbius laughs and projects another hologram. "YOU MEAN *THESE* FRIENDS?"

Mantastic shakes his head. "In order to be the #1 Hero Team, you're going to have to dethrone us. You think the world will believe the Fearless Five can be dethroned by your little playmates?"

Playmates? How old does he think I am?

"Not a chance," he says. "For this mission to work, we need the right kind of heroes."

Again, not cool. "The right kind of heroes? My friends are—"

"NOAH." Möbius floats closer. "THIS MISSION IS NOT ABOUT YOUR FRIENDS. IT IS ABOUT YOU— THE FATE OF THE WORLD DEPENDS ON YOU. . . . *YOU . . . YOU . . .*"

Everyone is silent. What do I say? I mean, if he's right, how can I say no?

"I heard that," says Mindstorm. "He's in!"

"Our hero!" Unicorn Magic blankets the room with confetti.

Spider Monkey applauds with all of his hands.

Mindstorm thinks to me, «*See, Noah? Courage.*»

Mantastic opens the door to my closet. Spider Monkey stuffs my belongings in with me.

"ONE LAST THING." Möbius has everyone's attention. "NO ONE, NOT EVEN YOUR NEW EPIC SUPER-TEAM, CAN KNOW THAT YOU PLAN TO SECURE THE SUPER STONE."

"They can't? Why not?" I ask.

"Think about it, Noah," says Mantastic. "Not all 'heroes' are heroes. All it takes is for one poser to hear the plan, and you'll be dead meat."

Rat squeaks, "And if your parents find out, you'll be double dead meat."

"Aaaagh! Get off me, Rat!"

Rat jumps out of the closet. Probably, hopefully.

"NOAH, DO YOU UNDERSTAND?" asks Möbius.

"Yeah, yeah. Keep my mouth shut, or I'm dead meat all over. Got it."

Mantastic holds out his fist for a bump. "Report to your closet for pickup at nine a.m."

I bump it. "No thanks. I'll walk."

"Whatever, dude." He closes me inside. Unicorn Magic sends me gliding home at a comfortable speed.

WHAT JUST HAPPENED?!

Everything is swirling around in my mind. Can I trust these people? This day has been totally off the rails. But I've gotta admit, I feel better than I have in a long time. Like I finally have a purpose. Like something is changing. Or starting. It feels good.

My closet glides to a stop.

My friends would flip if they knew where I just was. How the heck am I gonna keep this from them? From Mom and Dad? From Joy?

I open the closet door into my room.

Joy is floating in front of me. "Where were you?"

CHAPTER 9

Ninth Toilet on the Right

I kick my closet door shut behind me.

Joy squints, and the door swings open! A mountain of books, clothes, and random junk tumbles onto my bedroom floor.

"Your closet was gone for thirty-four and a half minutes. Where were you?"

"I heard you the first none-of-your-business time. Now get out of my room."

"Knock, knock." Mom walks in!

"Noah, honey, I . . . What on earth happened to your closet?"

"Ummm, I was, uhhh—"

Joy interrupts. "We're playing a game." She winks at me. "Ready, Noah?"

"Ready?" For what? What's she talking about? And since when does Joy wink?

My left arm rises in front of me. Then my right arm follows. Joy is controlling me like a puppet!

My right hand grips the sides of my watch, then Joy shouts, "Go!"

She makes my finger squeeze the timer. *BEEP.*

The junk on my floor leaps up, then flies into the closet. Coats hang themselves on hangers, old toys and board games arrange themselves on the shelf, shoes find their pairs and line up along the floor in front of neatly stacked library books.

Joy shouts, "Done!" and makes me stop the timer. *BEEP.* "How long that time, Noah?"

I'm totally confused, but I play along. "Oh, umm, seven seconds."

Joy's lips curl into a grin. "I win."

Mom claps. "I love it! Maybe you can play your game in the garage next."

Joy glares at me. "Noah likes to play games."

"Well, he can play all he wants now." Mom smiles. "You're not grounded."

"I'm not?"

"The Hall of Heroes called to apologize. The whole villain status thing was some kind of glitch."

"It was? I mean, yeah. It was! That explains it."

"I'm so sorry we didn't believe you. You're always honest with us."

Joy smirks. "Yeah, you're so honest."

I ignore her. "It's cool, Mom. No problem."

She turns to go, then stops in my doorway. "But, Noah, what was all that stuff about Professor Möbius?"

Crud. Think fast, Noah. "Umm, Möbius? Well, I . . ."

I look to Joy for help, but she's staring out my window. *CRASH! BEEEEP-BEEEEP-BEEEEP!*

Mom rushes to the window. "What's my car doing in the neighbor's tree?!" She hurries downstairs.

Joy drifts out my doorway without looking back. "Catch ya later, Noah." The door slams shut.

Seriously, she is so weird. And why did she help me? What's that little creeper up to?

You know when you wake up thinking it's an ordinary day, then remember it's Christmas or the first day of summer? This morning felt like that!

First, it's a Saturday, so no chance of school-induced dismemberment. Second, and much more important, I start my new life today. A life with a little control. Maybe even a little power!

My family's Saturday routine is hardwired into my neurons, so sneaking out of the house is easy. As for the Old Oaks Home, Friday nights are always wild, so I've got a few hours before I have to worry about Grandma and company.

I escape my neighborhood and head along the shoreline toward Half Dome. Overhead, the Fixers are flying home to nap before the usual Saturday-night super-battle blowout. The city is quiet right now, so I can walk down the street like a normal person. I pass a few fires and a toxic acid crater from last night, but otherwise the air is fresh and the sun is shining.

I hop the trolley on its way up to Half Dome. It's funny; I've seen the Hall of Heroes a thousand times, but today it looks different. It seems brighter somehow, even hopeful.

My phone buzzes. It's Arturo. He wants to know where I am. Man, I wish I could tell him. I ignore his message. It makes me feel a little sick, but it's better than lying.

I double-hop the steps up to the massive entrance. The doors are wide open. It's 9 a.m., but I'm not really sure where to go. Technically I work here now, so I guess I should just walk in.

I pass through the entrance into the lobby. It's the biggest room I've ever seen. Giant granite statues of the Fearless Five stretch up to a ginormous domed ceiling, so high I get dizzy looking up at it.

"Hey, kid!"

Mantastic swoops out of nowhere and lands in front of me.

"Hey, Mantas—"

"Sure, little boy!" Mantastic interrupts me. "I'd be happy to sign an autograph!"

"What?"

"Hi, Noah!" Unicorn Magic touches down with a wide horse smile. Mantastic shoots her a zip-it look.

She whispers, "Oh, right. Sorry," then raises her voice. "Noah! . . . No! . . . Ah! . . . No, aaannn autograph would be NO, AH, problem at all!" She winks at me and magically conjures up a pen and a notebook. She fumbles as she attempts to sign with her hoof.

I'm totally confused. "What's going on?"

Mantastic leans in with a toothy smile and whispers without moving his mouth, "What part of 'secret' didn't you understand?"

"But I didn't tell anybody."

"No, you just walked through the front door in broad daylight without a secret identity."

"I thought this *was* my secret identity."

Mantastic swipes the pad and pen from Unicorn Magic and scribbles a message. "Here ya go, kiddo!" he shouts. "What's that? You have to go pee-pee? Sure, sport, the potties are right over there."

Potties? He shoves the pad into my hands and pushes me off toward the restroom.

Magic waves. "See ya in a few, Noah! . . . NO! Uh, uh I don't know-uh if I'll ever see you again, stranger. Okay, bye-bye!" She streaks away in a puff of glitter.

I glance at the notepad and read, "The best kind of magic is LOVE. Love, Unicorn Magic xoxo." Beneath that: "Your new team is ready. Ninth toilet on the right. —The Fantastic Mantastic."

My team is in a toilet?

I step into the restroom. It's more like the Hall of Toilets. There must be a hundred stalls in here. I turn right and count until I get to the ninth stall. Maybe it's a secret entrance? I open the stall door.

Nope, just a toilet. Okay, now what? I step inside and close the door. Still nothing. I sit down on the lid. Am I supposed to just wait here for my team? *My team* that I don't even know. I guess I might like them. I mean, I like Unicorn Magic. And Mindstorm and Spider Monkey seem cool. Maybe my team will be more like them than Jerktastic.

"Having trouble in there, champ?!" Jerktastic's voice echoes from the restroom's entrance.

I yell, "I don't get it! What do you want me to do?"

"Having trouble flushing, are ya?" he says.

"Flushing?"

"Yeah, flushing! The toilet! With the button on the wall that flushes the toilet and doesn't do *anything else*!"

I stand up, turn, and hit the button on the wall. The toilet flushes, the stall shakes, then *DROPS!* It's an elevator! Or more like a free-fall carnival ride! It descends so fast I hover in midair as the toilet paper unrolls and flies to the ceiling.

DING! "Sublevel Five" says an elevator voice.

The stall jerks to a stop, sending me crashing to the floor.

The door opens. "Whoa, rough landing, dude." I feel a bunch of fuzzy hands lift me off the floor and stand me up. It's Spider Monkey. "Works way better if you stay seated."

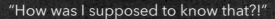

"How was I supposed to know that?!"

I hop out of the elevator, trying unsuccessfully to escape the web of toilet paper. I'm in a vast, dark room face to gigantic face with Professor Möbius.

"YOU'RE LATE! . . . *LATE* . . . *LATE* . . ."

"I'm not late. I've been here for like twenty minutes. Well, not here, but up–"

"You gotta be kiddin'! That dweeb is our leader?"

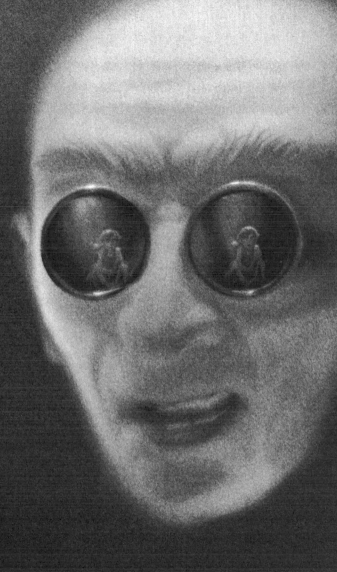

Crud, I know that voice. And
that stale locker-roomy smell.

CHAPTER 10

Brain vs. Brawn

Behind Möbius I see four familiar jerk-faces. The Magnificent Muscles.

Bone Head whines, "That loser? He's gonna make us look dumb."

"Dumb?" I fire back. "Have you looked in a mirror?"

Maximus chest-bumps me into Hit-Man, who flexes his pectorals of power, bouncing me to the floor in front of Catfight, who paws me back and forth like a toy mouse.

Mantastic laughs. "Okay, okay. Enough team bonding."

I scramble to my feet. "You call this bonding? There's no way they're on my team!"

Mantastic nods. "I know, I know. At first it didn't make sense to me either. You aren't exactly what the world looks for in a hero leader."

"I didn't mean me, I meant—"

"You aren't strong or good-looking, like the rest of us. But Professor Möbius is a genius, which means he has a genius plan!"

"A GENIUS PLAN, INDEED! FOR I SHALL BE THE TRUE GENIUS BEHIND THE FAKE GENIUS. NOTHING WILL BE REQUIRED OF NOAH, MENTALLY OR PHYSICALLY. NOTHING. ABSOLUTELY, POSITIVELY *NOTHING!*"

A spotlight clicks on, illuminating a full-body metallic super-suit and some sort of floating, high-tech chair.

Spider Monkey tosses the suit to me. It opens in mid-air and wraps itself around my body. A face-covering helmet clamps over my head, then clicks into the suit as the chair scoops me up from behind.

"MUSCLES, MEET YOUR NEW, FAKE LEADER–
DR. BRAIN-MAN!"

Dr. Brain-Man?

"Wow!" Maximus is impressed. "Dweeb looks pretty cool. So you're sayin' no one will ever see his face?"

"No one," Mantastic assures him.

"Awesome! Let's do this thing!"

"NO!" I shout.

The speaker system in the suit changes my voice, making me sound like a cross between Optimus Prime and Darth Vader. "No! Let's not do this! I don't want these jerks on my team!"

The room is silent.

"Dweeb sounds awesome!" says Catfight.

"Yeah, he sounds epic!" says Hit-Man.

"Say more stuff, dweeb!" says Bone Head.

"NO!" I shout in my amazing voice. "You welded me inside a locker!"

"Hey, Dr. Dweeb-Man, say my name with your cool voice! Say 'Awesomus Maximus'!" The rest of the Muscles jump in with similar requests.

Mantastic pulls me aside. "Listen, bro, I know you don't like these guys, but we need a team that can go all the way. And they're, well, they're like me. And the world loves me, right?"

I want to say, "Not *everyone* in the world loves you!" but I'm afraid I'll sound so incredibly cool he won't catch the insult. Instead I shake my helmet.

"Come on, even you thought I was great until you met me, right?"

Good point.

"You gotta trust me, Noah. I know what I'm doing." He raises his fist for a bump.

I stare at his hand. I'm not sure I trust him, so I leave it unbumped. All I can muster is "Whatever, let's go."

Unfortunately, my Dr. Brain-Man voice makes my "Whatever, let's go" sound like an inspirational battle cry. The Muscles parrot me, "YEAH! Whatever! Let's goooo!"

Mantastic slaps me on the back. "Yeah, bro, that's it! Whatever! Let's GOOOO!"

Suddenly, light floods the room—which isn't really a room. It's more like an underground world! Several city blocks are replicated in detail with robotic people, cars, heroes, villains, and news crews.

"WELCOME TO THE HALL OF HEROES HERO TRAINING HALL!"

My ears are ringing. Möbius's voice is even louder through my suit's speakers.

"DR. BRAIN-MAN," blares Möbius, "YOUR JOB IS SIMPLE—GLIDE AROUND ON YOUR GENIUSLY DESIGNED CHAIR, PRETEND TO BE IN CHARGE, AND TRY NOT TO DIE."

"Try not to *die*?"

"MUSCLES," Möbius shouts, "WHATEVER! LET'S GOOOO! . . . *GOOOO* . . . *GOOOO* . . . "

The Muscles rush into the fake city, attacking every fake villain like dogs unleashed in a ball factory.

Möbius yells, "DR. BRAIN-MAN, GET MOVING! MAKE CERTAIN THE MUSCLES ARE IN FRONT OF THE NEWS CAMERAS WHEN THE SPIDER INVASION BEGINS."

"The spider invasion? Wait a sec—" But my hover-chair zooms me into the simulation! "Aaaagh!"

«Hi, Noah! I mean . . . Hello, Dr. Brain-Man!»

«Mindstorm, is that you?»

«Yep! I'm gonna establish a mind link so you can talk to your team! Here we go. Mind link ON!»

Suddenly, my brain is flooded with a stream of Muscle thoughts about flexing for the fake news cameras, taking the enemy to the "gun show," whether or not they applied enough spray tan. . . .

Inside my helmet, the heads-up display tracks every possible threat with tiny red triangles and useless scrolling data. Then, "WARNING! WARNING!" I'm seconds from crashing into a building!

I scream, "How do I control this thing?!"

"WITH THE CONTROLS, OF COURSE," says Möbius.

Controls? I look past the display nonsense and scan the chair. The armrest has about a hundred glowing buttons. Four of them are arrows.

I hit the left arrow. My chair banks left and scrapes along a building.

"SLOPPY BUT EFFECTIVE, DR. BRAIN-MAN. NOW LET US BEGIN!"

Begin?! I was hoping we were almost done!

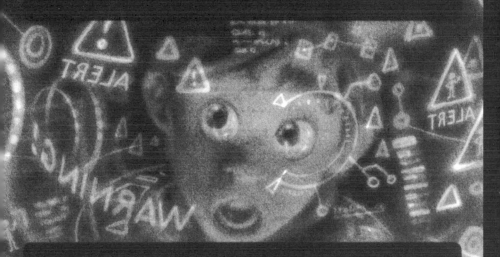

«You crack me up, bro.» Mantastic laughs over the jumble of Muscles in my head. *«Ready or not, here come the spiders!»*

I scan the walls, the ground!

BOOM! Buildings and signs shudder. The fake people shake and bounce like bobblehead dolls.

BOOM! Long shadows crawl across the skyline. *CRUNCH!* Gigantic metal legs crash through rooftops, crushing water towers and billboards!

Cars and buses tumble as Mantastic and Magic pilot giant mechanical spiders through the fake city.

"BEHOLD THE MAIN EVENT!" Möbius's voice thunders over the warning alerts in my helmet. "ASSEMBLE THE MAGNIFICENT MUSCLES IN FRONT OF THE NEWS CAMERAS AND COMMENCE YOUR HERO MONOLOGUING."

How am I supposed to do anything when my out-of-control chair is bouncing like a pinball through the streets? WARNING! . . . DANGER! . . . CRITICAL! . . . SYSTEM FAILURE! . . . ODDS OF SURVIVAL: 19% . . . 17% . . . 5% . . .

I yank off my helmet and chuck it. I can see again! *I can see* a fake helicopter with real blades spinning toward my unprotected head!

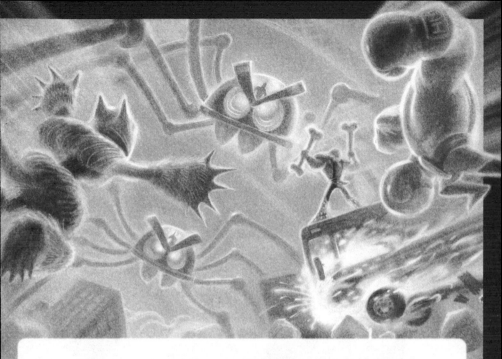

I smash the DOWN button on the console! The chair dives below the blades. I lose an inch of hair off the top, but my head is still attached!

I hit the UP button and rocket above the simulation. Now I have a bird's-eye view:

The Muscles are schoolyard-brawl-style punching, kicking and scratching the giant spider legs. The mind link is a torrent of trash-talk, bad one-liners, and incoherent spider puns. It's like the Muscles think they're in the final battle of their own superhero movie. But from up here they look more like Chihuahuas chasing down monster trucks.

I mind-shout down to them, «*Guys! This isn't like stealing my lunch money! I've got an idea. If we work together, we can—*»

Möbius interjects, «*DR. BRAIN-MAN, I ASSUMED IT WAS OBVIOUS THAT HERO-MONOLOGUING MUST BE SPOKEN ALOUD TO BE OF ANY PUBLIC RELATIONS BENEFIT.*»

«*I'm not monologuing!*» I nosedive into the fight. «*Listen, these things are big, but they're top-heavy. If we can make a giant trip wire—*»

Hit-Man interrupts. «*Trip wire? Is that some lame Old World thing? I'm Hit-Man. I don't trip—I HIIIIT!*» *KLANG KLANG KLANG!* Hit-Man lands a few useless blows on a spider leg before it flicks him through a shopping mall.

«*Hitting won't work on these things!*» I zoom down between the giant spider legs, then over to a telephone pole. «*You guys, rip out these power lines, then tie them together and string them between the buildings!*»

«*Catfight, those fake clouds up there are made of canvas. If we can tear them down, we can wrap them around the spiders' heads like blindfolds—*»

«*Sorry, Brain-Fart!*» shouts Maximus. «*Your lame Old World plan is lame and old. Plus, we're totally winning! See all the destruction and explosions? And if you wanna talk, use the suit so we don't have to hear your dweeb voice! Ready, Muscles? WHATEVER! LET'S GOOOO!*»

The Muscles rush the spiders. It's a ludicrous free-for-all: zero strategy, zero sense, zero chance of success. Buildings crash like waves around me!

I kick my chair into high gear and jet through the chaos like a surfer shooting the tube. The wave is closing . . . closing . . . getting tighter . . . tighter . . . not gonna make it . . . not gonna . . .

I pop out the end as the last building crashes in my wake! Woo-hoo! I did it! I'm starting to get the hang of this thing!

WHAM! I'm slammed from behind by a flying phone booth! I tumble end over end into a cloud of falling debris. . . .

Everything goes DARK.

«*Noah? Noah, are you okay?*» Mindstorm's voice snaps my brain back online.

I open my dust-coated eyes. I'm lying in a pile of rubble with the Five and the Muscles standing over me.

"Magical effort!" Unicorn pats me on the head with her hoof. Owwww.

Mantastic is shaking his head, "Well, you managed to destroy everything but the spiders. Epic fail, bruh."

"Total epic fail," adds Maximus. "Nathan is clearly the problem."

Mantastic puts his hand on my shoulder. "His name is Noah." Then he turns to Maximus. "But yeah, he's clearly the problem."

"What?!" I cough up a cloud of pulverized concrete. "*I'm* the problem?"

"EXACTLY. WE ARE ALL IN AGREEMENT," says Möbius. "NOAH IS THE PROBLEM. FORTUNATELY I AM A GENIUS, SO I HAVE A GENIUS SOLUTION: I WILL REVISE NOAH'S HELMET—IT WILL BE UN-REMOVABLE, AND HIS CHAIR AND SUIT WILL BE REMOTE-CONTROLLABLE."

"You're gonna make me a remote-control puppet?"

"PRECISELY! ENSURING YOUR LACK OF INTELLECT AND COORDINATION POSE NO

THREAT TO OUR BRILLIANT PLAN."

Mantastic loves the idea. "Total upgrade, Noah! You can take a nap during missions if you want!"

If I want?! What I *want* is to say NO. I *want* to yell, to scream, to blame them! But what's the point? Nothing I say matters.

Magic waves her hoof. My closet zooms in and stops in front of me.

Spider Monkey collapses my mech-suit and helps me inside. "Dude, that was some gnarly chair-surfing at the end." I know he's trying to be nice, but I don't care. I just want to leave.

Mantastic nudges my cheek with his hulking fist. "Don't feel bad, Noah. Next time we'll guarantee you don't screw up."

Seriously, how can a "hero" be so clueless? But then I see Unicorn Magic behind his shoulder. She's looking right at me. She seems concerned—for me, I think. Maybe she understands what I'm feeling. My eyes tear up—

Bad time to cry! I pull my closet door shut before Mantastic sees.

I sink into the corner as my closet flies home. I wish it would just keep going. I don't want to get anywhere right now. I don't want to do anything or see anybody. I just want to fly away forever.

But my closet just stopped.

CHAPTER 11

The New Team

I don't know how long I've been sitting here in the dark. Maybe ten minutes. Maybe thirty. I open my closet door—

Joy is hovering there again!

Before she can say a word, I give her the "not now" hand gesture and walk out of my room.

I have dozens of unread texts from my friends. They're worried about me. See what I mean? *They* should be my team. They actually care about me. Plus, they know my name! I want so badly to tell them what's going on, not that they could fix anything. I just wish I wasn't so alone. And I feel like a total jerk for keeping them in the dark.

I pass Mom and Dad in the kitchen. Mom says something to me, but I pretend I don't hear and head straight for the garage. I can't do family right now.

I pull open a wooden door to what used to be a storage space. Now it conceals a lead-core, carbon-fiber blast door. I swing it open and head downstairs to my bunker.

Yup, you heard me right; my parents built me a safety bunker thirty feet beneath the house. It can withstand most super-assaults, at least for a little while. If my parents had their way, I'd stay down here twenty-four/ seven. So to bribe me, they let me outfit it with anything I want. My friends and I call it the Fortress of Chillitude

because it's basically a biosphere of awesomeness, packed with stuff people used to like before the meteorite: foosball, Donkey Kong, beanbag chairs, and posters of movies that have *nothing* to do with superheroes.

As I reach the bottom of the stairs . . .

"NOAH!"

"Aagh!" I'm startled and slip down the last steps. "Geez, you guys scared the crud out of me."

My friends jump up from the couch and beanbags. Arturo helps me off the floor. "Dude, we've been trying to find you all day."

Ivy grabs my hand. She can always sense when something's wrong. "You're hurt. What happened?"

I hadn't even noticed my broken thumb. As Ivy

heals me, Tabitha peppers me with questions. "Where were you? What's going on? Are you in some sort of trouble?"

The more I don't answer, the more everyone presses me. Honestly, at this point, I don't know why I'm not telling them.

"Okay, okay! But you've gotta keep it secret. Like really, really secret."

"You got it. Lips sealed. Totally vaulted," they say.

Ivy lets go of my hand; my thumb is good as new. "Noah, just tell us."

"You aren't gonna believe this, but I've been recruited by . . ."

I spot Joy listening at the top of the staircase! I hit the panic button on my desk. The blast door slams shut, locking the little spy outside. Man, that was close.

I launch into a stream-of-consciousness info dump. About ninety seconds later, I finish the world's longest run-on sentence containing every detail of my apocalyptic secret. I take a deep breath while my friends process everything.

Arturo bursts out laughing. "Man, for a minute, I totally believed you."

Ivy smacks his shoulder without taking her eyes off me. "He's telling the truth."

Arturo's jaw drops as he processes it all a second time. "Soooo . . . you really have to save the world? With the Meatheads? Hey, wait a second. *We're* your team!"

Hugh grows in anger and size. "Yeah, your team is us!"

Tabitha adds, "We always have your back!"

Ivy interrupts. "You guys, I don't think it's up to him. Is it, Noah?"

"No. That's the problem. I'm totally stuck and there's nothing I can do. Professor Möbius—"

BLING-A-BLING-A-BLING! The TV flickers on—it's a video call. From Professor Möbius!

"Hurry! Hide! Hide! And keep quiet!"

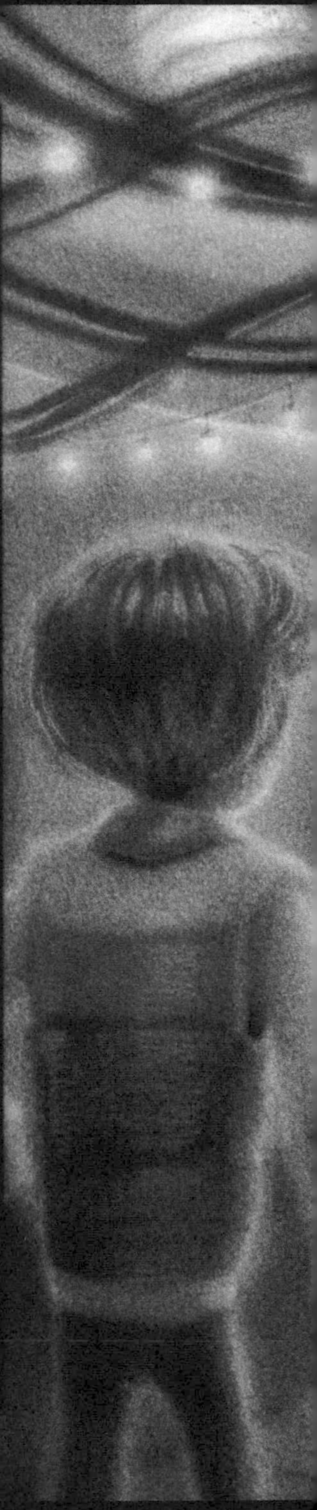

My friends dive for cover as Möbius's head fills the screen. "GREETINGS, DR. BRAIN-MAN!"

Arturo mouths, "Dr. Brain-Man?" I shoot him a look that clearly means "Shut it."

I play it cool. "Hey, Professor."

"ARE YOU READY TO MAKE HISTORY?"

"Am I ready to make history?"

"YES. WAIT, ARE YOU ASKING ME? I WAS ASKING YOU."

"What?"

"I WAS ASKING YOU IF YOU ARE READY TO MAKE HISTORY."

"Okay."

"OKAY, YOU ARE READY? OR OKAY YOU UNDERSTAND THAT I WAS ASKING YOU?"

Arturo is struggling to keep his laugh in his face. I've gotta speed this up. "So, what's going on, Professor?"

"EXCITING STUFF! IT IS TIME FOR YOUR FIRST MISSION!"

"What, already? A real mission? With real villains? Are you joking?"

"I DO NOT JOKE. WE'VE BEEN OVER THIS. ANYHOW, DR. DESTRUCTO IS—"

"Whoa, whoa, whoa! Our first mission involves Dr. Destructo? Like #1 Villain Dr. Destructo?"

"EXACTLY! CAN YOU BELIEVE OUR LUCK? DESTRUCTO-TROOPERS ARE INVADING POWERDISE ISLAND AS WE SPEAK! THEIR VILLAIN MASTERMIND CANNOT BE FAR BEHIND. THIS IS THE PERFECT OPPORTUNITY FOR YOUR TEAM TO PROVE ITSELF TO THE WORLD!"

The word "team" turns Hugh's face red. He expands, cracking his hide-a-cubby. Tabitha acts fast, lassoing the cubby and squeezing Hugh back down to size.

"SPEAKING OF YOUR TEAM, THEY SHOULD BE ON THIS CALL. WHERE ARE THOSE MARVELOUS MUSCLES?"

Arturo mouths, "Marvelous Muscles?" I look to Tabitha for help. She nods, then ropes Arturo's mouth shut.

"Yeah, about *that,*" I say. "Can we talk about my team?"

"I COULD TALK ABOUT THE MAGNIFICENT MUSCLES ALL DAY, BUT RIGHT NOW WE HAVE—"

WHAM! WHAM! The room rattles.

Möbius stops, "WHAT WAS *THAT?*"

WHAM! WHAM! WHAM! Joy is pounding on the blast door!

"WHAT IS THAT NOISE?"

"Oh, uhh, just a battle outside. You know how it is. Anyway, about that mission, I don't think we're ready. I mean, our training was pretty catastrophic."

"WE ARE IN COMPLETE AGREEMENT. YOU, NOAH, ARE NOT READY FOR ANY MISSION. FORTUNATELY, I HAVE MADE THE NECESSARY UPGRADES TO YOUR SUIT AND CHAIR. YOU WILL FIND THEM IN YOUR CLOSET. ASSEMBLE YOUR GLORIOUS TEAM AND RENDEZVOUS WITH THE FIVE AT POWERDISE ISLAND!"

Ivy shakes her head.

A deep, metal-bending sound reverberates from the top of the stairs just as the Muscles pop onto the video call.

"Sorry we're late." Maximus flexes for his webcam. "We were oiling our muscles. What's the sitch?"

"EXCELLENT, YOU ARE OILED UP AND READY TO GO! DR. BRAIN-MAN WILL BRIEF YOU ON YOUR FIRST MISSION." Möbius signs off.

"Sweet sauce! Our first mission!" Maximus and the Muscles chest-bump and headbutt each other.

KLANG! KLANG! KLANG! The blast door tumbles down the staircase!

Maximus is too busy sculpting his hair with his greasy hand to notice. "Don't just sit there, loser. Tell us the plan."

I glance around the room at my friends. They're frustrated, a little hurt, a lot angry. But mostly worried about me.

"Right, umm, the plan . . . ," I say.

Maximus smacks his phone as if it's me. "Spit it out, Dr. Brain-Dead!"

Okay, time to rally my team. I shoot Ivy a sly grin. Her eyes go wide; she knows I'm up to something.

"Listen up, Muscles, we've got a triple-code-red emergency at the Old Oaks Home. Get down there ASAP! I'll be right behind you."

"*Pfff,* don't bother, waste of space. You'll just be in the way." Maximus poke-poke-pokes at his phone with his oily finger, trying to hang up. Eight pokes later, the screen goes black.

My friends gawk at me with loose jaws.

I smile. "Grandma will keep 'em busy for a while. So, who's ready to be the world's new #1 Hero Team?"

"YEEEAAAAAAAAH!" Hugh goes big, obliterating the cubby. Replay generates a cheering Madden NFL crowd and does a little dance. Tabitha gives hair hugs and high fives to everybody at the same time. Yeah, they're a weird team. But they're my team!

We rush to the staircase, but Joy is blocking it. "What's going on?"

"Hi, Joy." "Hi, Joy." "Hi, Joy." My friends squeeze past her and race up the stairs.

I smirk. "You know, just playing a game."

Tabitha casts a hair rope like a lifeline and hoists me over Joy and up the stairs.

I grin at Joy from the mangled doorway. "You'd better fix this before Mom sees."

CHAPTER 12

Trouble in Powerdise

My friends and I roar through the sky, ten thousand feet above the water, in a video game fighter jet spawned by Arturo.

Watching the ocean always soothes my nerves. Too bad it doesn't soothe my stomach, because I am all kinds of airsick right now. Focus, Noah. Focus. MUST . . . NOT . . . TOSS . . . COOKIES.

When California was cracked off into the Pacific, a new body of water was formed called the Gulf of Supercalifornevada. The resulting volcanic activity created a landmass named Powerdise Island. That's where we're headed.

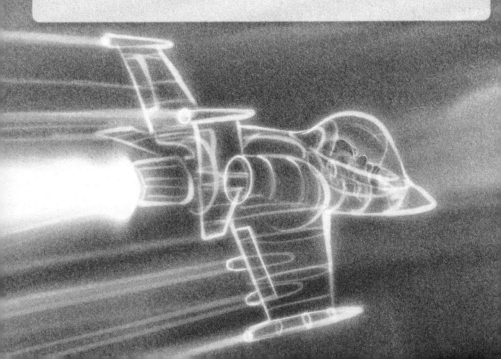

My friends are pumped. Hugh and Tabitha are running through hero-monologue options while Ivy studies Powerdise maps and photos using the onboard computer.

Arturo does his captain voice. "As we begin our descent, please be sure your seat back is in the upright position, your tray table is put away, and Noah's barf bag is securely stowed in . . . What the . . . ? You guys, look!"

Powerdise Island comes into view on the horizon.

"That doesn't look at all like the photos." Ivy punches some buttons and brings up the news feeds from the island.

The livestream footage looks like a swarm of killer bees fighting a thousand fireflies at a laser show in a fireworks factory.

At the top of the volcano, hundreds of Destructo-Troopers are installing lots of weird, evil-looking machinery.

On the volcano's slopes, hordes of Troopers battle frenzied heroes, causing a super-brain chain reaction to spread like a bad rash.

From hillside to poolside to seaside, vacationing heroes and villains are ditching their tropical drinks to join the super-mobs rampaging through every hotel, cruise ship, and barefoot bar on the island!

I can see my friends are getting sucked in too. They've switched into their super-suits and Hugh is already triple size. I've gotta reel them back in!

"Ivy, turn off the news feeds!" But she doesn't.

Hugh has a tear in his oversized eye. "But it's so beautiful."

I rush to the console and turn off the screen.

"Guys, look at me! Over here, look! Don't fall for the super-nonsense. We've got a job to do!"

"Yeah." Arturo lights up. "We've gotta kick some villain butt!"

"No! We have to defeat the world's #1 Villain in front of news cameras. That's our job. Our only job. See all those heroes down there? None of them are going to stop Destructo because they're all super-crazed right now. The more they 'kick villain butt,' the more Destructo wins! Get it?"

Years of my non-super speeches have given my friends the ability to resist super-brain. Ivy shakes her head like she's trying to wake up. "Noah's right, you guys."

Wahoo, Ivy's back!

Tabitha and Hugh follow. Then even Arturo. "All right, Dr. No Fun, what's the plan?"

"The plan? Right. I don't actually have a—"

«Noah?» Mindstorm's voice fills my head. *«Everything's ready now—heavy fighting, hopeless situation, news cameras. It's perfect! Where are you?»*

I think back to her, *«Oh, hey, Mindstorm. Umm, we're almost there. Where are you?»*

«We're in the Justice Jet, ready to rendezvous with you and your team.»

"Noah? Hellooooo?" Tabitha pokes my forehead with a hair tentacle because I haven't said a word out loud for about fifteen seconds. "Anybody there?"

"Oh, right. Sorry. I'm talking to Mindstorm with my brain. Telepathically."

Her eyes shift to my forehead. "Cooooool."

«Noah, who are you talking to? I can't sense your team. Are they with you?»

Uh-oh, I've got some explaining to do. *«Right. My team. So, about my team—»*

"WARNING!" the cockpit computer blares.

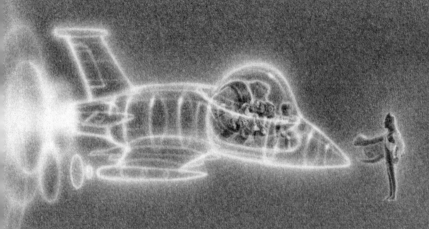

Arturo stops the jet in midair, hurling us to the floor. My lunch is about to . . .

"Noah, where's your *suit*?!" I look out the windshield. Mantastic is hovering right in front of us. "And where's your *team*?!"

My friends are frozen with starstruckness. Hugh whispers, "Dude, Mantastic knows your name."

I pick myself up off the floor as I choke down my queasiness. Here goes. "My team? Yeah, umm, *this* is my team."

My friends smile and wave.

Mantastic's eyes glow red, which probably means he's trying to keep his eye lasers from blowing a hole through my head.

Unicorn Magic slides up on a rainbow. "Oooh, Dr. Brain-Man, I loooove your new team! I wanna be your first fan!"

Tabitha whispers, "Unicorn Magic. It's Unicorn Magic. She wants to be our FAN."

Mantastic interrupts. "Hold your sparkles, Magic. This mission is over!"

Over? What's he talking about? "Wait! I know we aren't your idea of an A-team, but trust me, these guys are amazing! Let us prove it."

Magic claps her hooves. "Great idea, Doctor! That's why you're the Brain-Man."

"A-team?" Mantastic laughs. "You're not even a B- or C-team. You're barely a Z-team!"

Mantastic just lost four more fans. Arturo is about to throw down Mortal Kombat–style! I grab his arm. "Stay cool."

Mantastic cracks his knuckles. "You wanna go, Game Boy?"

Magic interrupts. "Listen, everyone, why don't we try the twelve L's of conflict resolution?"

"What's that?" Ivy asks.

"The twelve L's are Loving, Listening, L—"

"I'm sorry, Magic, I meant what's *THAT*?!"

Ivy points at the clouds above the island. A gigantic metal *something* emerges with Dr. Destructo riding on it!

"WHOA," we all say in unison.

"He upsized again!" says Tabitha.

Hugh is in awe. "He makes me look like a tiny action figure."

Ominous villain music fills the air like a movie score.

Destructo lowers the strange machine onto the island's volcano, sealing the crater. The machine whirs to life; a giant cannon telescopes out and starts to pump lava from the volcano!

Streams of molten rock and iron blast from the double-barreled lava cannon, splashing over a line of beachfront resorts. The buildings are washed away in a river of fire!

Screaming heroes and villains flee in terror—not play hero terror—*ACTUAL TERROR!*

Magic gasps. "Can super-people survive being buried in lava?" She doesn't wait for an answer. "We've gotta get down there!" *«Mindstorm!»* she mind-shouts.

«Right here!»

Above us, the Justice Jet roars to a midair stop! Mindstorm leaps out of the airlock. Monkey follows in his flying-monkey winged vest.

«Mindstorm,» Magic continues. *«Can you still locate people if they're buried under lava?»*

«Totally!»

Mantastic turns to Spider Monkey. "They're gonna need all the hands they can get. I'll take care of Destructo!"

Monkey, Magic, and Mindstorm streak toward the action.

My friends turn to me. They're keyed up—dying to be set loose. But this time it's not super-brain, they just want to help.

"Mantastic!" I shout. "Please, you've gotta let my friends—"

"Sorry, bro. Things just got real. I wouldn't even let the Muscles near this fight." He looks right at Ivy. "Rat, get these kids into the jet and keep them there!"

"So now I'm the babysitter?"

"Aaaah!" Ivy screams. "He's on my shoulder!"

Mantastic rockets toward the top of the volcano. The Invisible Rat bites, scratches, and tail-whips us into the Justice Jet like a creepy phantom sheepdog.

"Ouch!" "Aaaaaghh!" "It's in my hair!" My friends huddle behind me for protection. This is definitely a first.

We watch the battle raging through the windows. The jet's video monitors display the news coverage, plus I'm hearing a play-by-play through the mind link as . . .

In a hailstorm of psionic-confusion blasts and rainbow rays, Mindstorm and Magic blitz the ranks of Destructo-Troopers and streak toward the coastline.

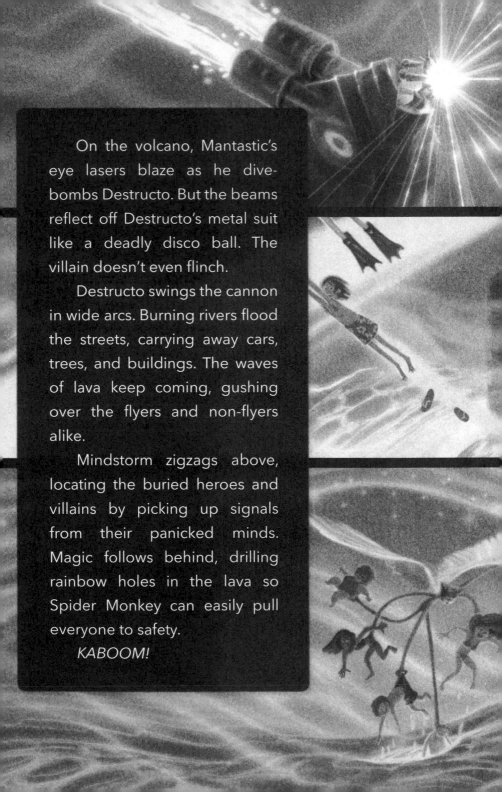

On the volcano, Mantastic's eye lasers blaze as he dive-bombs Destructo. But the beams reflect off Destructo's metal suit like a deadly disco ball. The villain doesn't even flinch.

Destructo swings the cannon in wide arcs. Burning rivers flood the streets, carrying away cars, trees, and buildings. The waves of lava keep coming, gushing over the flyers and non-flyers alike.

Mindstorm zigzags above, locating the buried heroes and villains by picking up signals from their panicked minds. Magic follows behind, drilling rainbow holes in the lava so Spider Monkey can easily pull everyone to safety.

KABOOM!

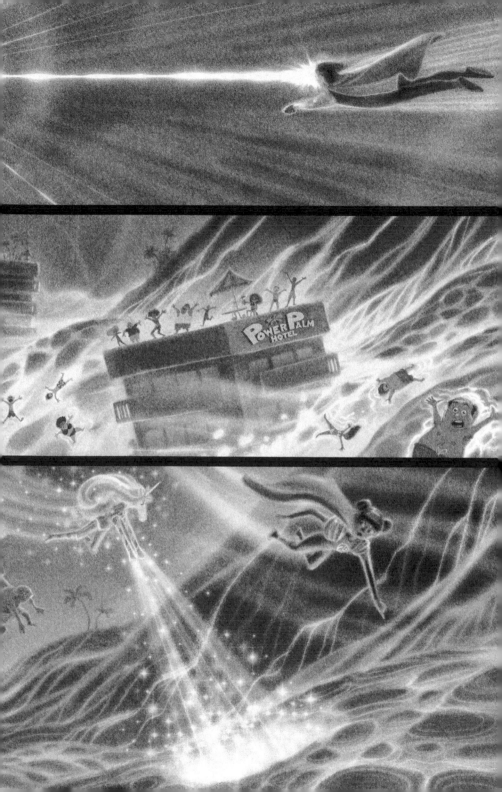

A sonic boom echoes off the ocean as Mantastic rockets straight at Destructo's chest. *KLANG!* Mantastic ricochets like a bullet off Superman. But it works! Destructo falls!

I scan the volcano's slope for Mantastic, but the smoke is heavy and the unmanned cannon is flinging ribbons of lava wildly in every direction!

«*Mantastic!*» I mind-shout. «*Where are you? Are you okay?*»

«*Super.*» Mantastic emerges from the smoke, rubbing his head. Destructo rockets up behind him and lands on the cannon!

As Mantastic backs up for another shot, Destructo pulls a massive lever on the cannon. The lava stream stops and the cannon pulses. The pulsing accelerates . . . *faster* . . . *FASTER* . . . *LOUDER!* The whole island trembles like an earthquake!

KABOOOOOM!

Another sonic boom as Mantastic rockets toward Destructo, but the villain swings around and—*KLANG*—catches Mantastic in a giant metal bear hug. They plummet into a cloud of ash.

BOOOOM! The volcano erupts, swallowing the cannon in a column of fire and lava.

"WARNING! WARNING!" Lights flash and sirens blare inside the jet. The mind link is a jumble of terror and panic.

A holographic video display lights up in front of us, showing a wide view of the volcano. Rat-sized handprints frantically zoom the video and swipe this way and that, searching, searching. . . .

I point. "There!"

Rat zooms in. Monkey and Mindstorm are pulling people behind Unicorn Magic as she generates a rainbow wall. A tidal wave of lava crashes against the wall, then over it, burying everyone alive!

Ivy grabs my wrist. "They need help!"

«Mindstorm!» I mind-shout. «Are you there?!»

«I'm here.» She sounds faint. «Rat . . . keep Noah . . . safe.»

Arturo runs to the hatch. "Noah, if we can locate them beneath the lava, we can save them!"

«Mindstorm! I'll stay here, but please, you've gotta link in my friends!»

There's no response. Arturo's impatient. "Are you guys brain-talking? This is so confusing. Nobody's saying anything!"

«Mindstorm, it's Rat! Noah's got a point. His team has a Fixer, a giant, a materializer, and a . . . umm . . . person who can juggle people with her hair.»

The mind link is silent. My friends' eyes are locked on me, waiting for an answer.

They startle as Mindstorm's voice fills their heads. «Welcome to the show.»

My friends fill the link with a flurry of cheers! «WOO-HOO!» «YEEESS!» «We're in!»

All except Hugh, who can't stop giggling. "My brain tickles!"

CHAPTER 13
Powerdise Lost

Rat opens the airlock. My friends rush to the door, look each other in the eyes, nod, then LEAP!

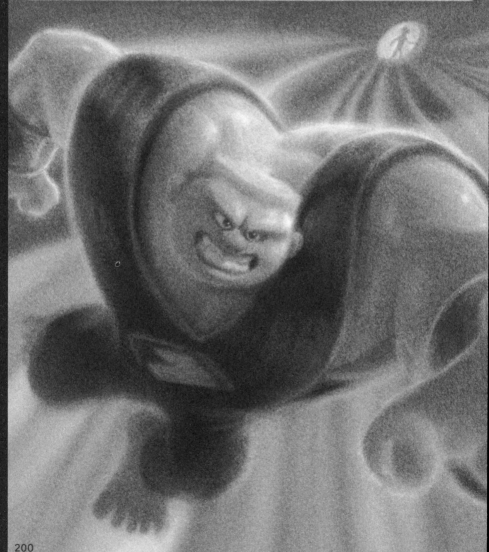

Rat turns to me (I assume) and squeaks, "Noah, stay here!"

"I'm five thousand feet in the air. Where am I gonna go?"

I swipe and zoom the video screen, tracking my amazing friends as they storm into the action!

Hugh-Mongous, Nightingale, and Rat head off to rescue anyone still above the lava. Hugh-Mongous pushes a building over, creating a giant life raft. Nightingale flies ahead, pulling people aboard and repairing the building as it burns. Rat uses his creepy wrangling skills to keep everyone on board.

Replay and Hairstrike fly over the flowing lava in a Fortnite glider. There's a lot of cross-talk on the mind link, but I hear Hairstrike. «Mindstorm? Hello? Are you there?»

«I'm here!»

«Oh, yay! Hi! Nice to meet you. My name is Tabitha. Actually, technically, right now I'm Hairstrike. Anyway, I'm a huge fan!»

«Tabitha!» I mind-shout. «Focus!»

«I am focused! Anyway, Mindstorm, we can see where— Actually, we can't really see where you are, but we can feel your location. Seriously, this mind link stuff is awesomeness! And bizarre. Anyway, you guys are under about thirty feet of lava right now and there's no way we can get through—»

«What?!» Rat interrupts. «You said you had a plan!»

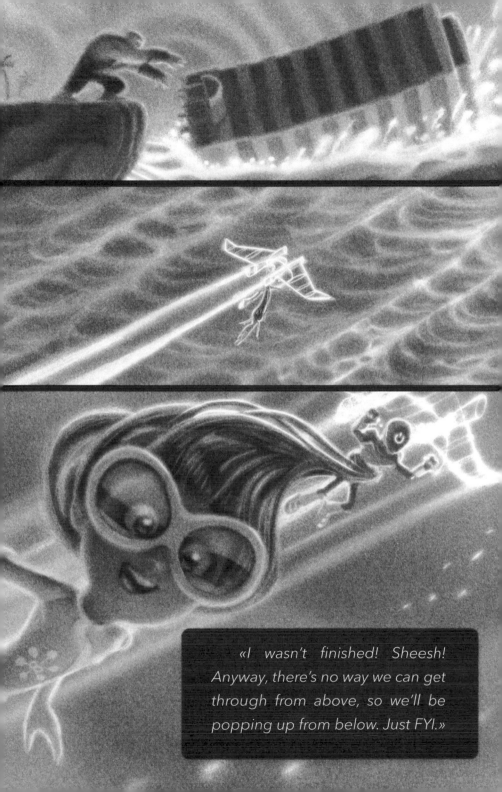

«I wasn't finished! Sheesh! Anyway, there's no way we can get through from above, so we'll be popping up from below. Just FYI.»

Replay and Hairstrike dive-bomb an open stretch of beach. Seconds before impact, Replay's glider transforms into the digging suit, helmet, and shovel from the classic video game Dig Dug. Replay's shovel incinerates the ground on contact, creating a perfectly round tunnel. He and Hairstrike disappear into the earth!

Wahoo! Z-team, my butt! Wait, where's Mantastic?

I swipe the screen and zoom in to the top of the volcano, but it's hard to make anything out through the fire and smoke.

«Mantastic? MANTASTIC?!»

I strain to listen through the chaotic mind link. Then I hear his voice, soft and weak. *«Doin' . . . awesome, bro. . . . Got Destructo right . . . where . . .»*

On the screen, I see a silhouette in the fire. It's Dr. Destructo! He's at the edge of the volcano, holding Mantastic in the lava stream!

Mantastic needs help! I've gotta do something.

«Noah!» Mantastic's voice fills my head. *«Don't you . . . dare!»*

Dang, the mind link! He's reading my thoughts!

«Noah . . . You are more important . . . than any of us. . . . You . . . must . . .»

But I can't just let him die!

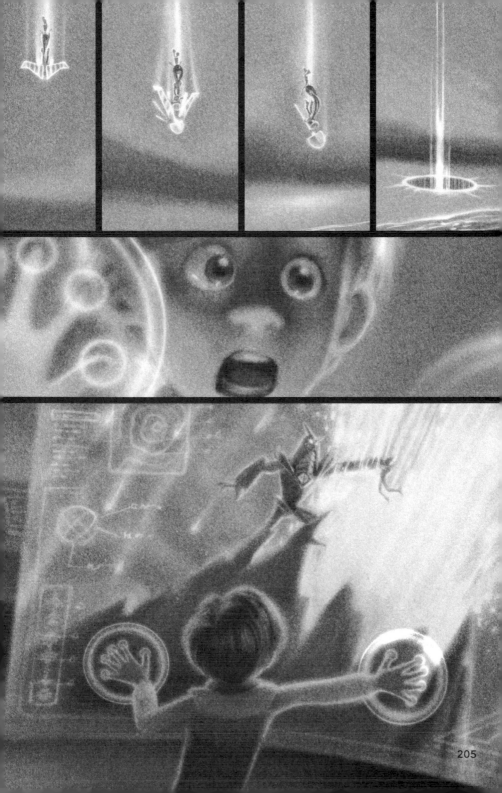

205

«*Noah.*» It's Magic. «*We'll save Mantastic when we get out from under this lava. In the meantime, just sit tight, okay?*»

«*No, it'll be too late! But what can I do? I'm stuck here in this jet. . . . In this massive metal jet . . . filled with ANTIMATTER ROCKET FUEL!*»

«*NOAH!*» The link is flooded with protesting shouts, but I don't care. I swing the screen around. Ivy, Hugh, and Rat are almost to the ocean on their building-raft.

I run to the front of the plane. The cockpit is lit up with a thousand buttons, dials, gauges, and a stick thingy. I push the stick forward. The jet nose-dives! Whoa! I pull it back. The jet levels. I see a handle that goes forward and backward. A throttle maybe? I push it. I jet forward . . . then sideways. Uh-oh, *too sideways*! I course correct. Make that *overcorrect*! I level out. Sort of.

«*Rat! I need Nightingale and Hugh-Mongous. Can you keep those people on the raft till they reach the ocean?*»

«*I have invisible teeth, don't I?*»

«*Hugh, you need to hop on the jet as I pass by!*»

«*SWEET!*»

«*Ivy, follow right behind. This only works if we have a Fixer!*»

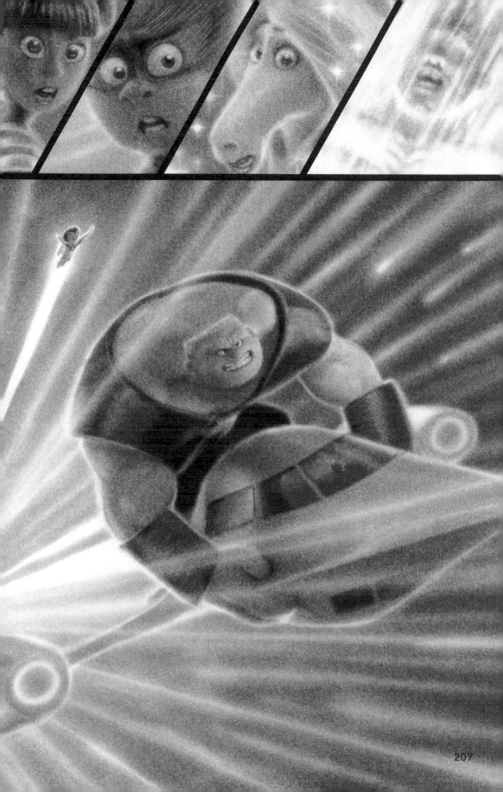

207

CRUNCH! The jet drops fifteen feet, then levels again. «Hey, buddy!» Hugh is on the roof!

«Ivy, you here too?»

«Right behind you. But, Noah, I can't fix you if you blow up in a jet. INSIDE A VOLCANO!»

«You won't have to as long as Hugh can catch!»

«I can totally catch! Sometimes!»

The jet twists and turns as I attempt to angle it toward the top of the volcano and Dr. Destructo. I put everything out of my mind—the shouting voices, the fact that my stomach wants to eject its contents onto the windshield. Just focus . . . focus . . . on . . . Destructo. . . .

"WARNING! WARNING!" We're about to crash into something big!

Up ahead, Dr. Destructo's arms glow red as he holds Mantastic's motionless body in the stream of fire. Even super molecules can't stand up to that heat!

I stumble back to the airlock and throw it open. Scorching wind and the smell of burning earth blow me back. I grit my teeth. Here goes. I push forward. Push . . . push . . . then . . .

CHAPTER 14

The Z-Team

The whole world was watching.

But they didn't see me.

They saw Hugh-Mongous riding the Justice Jet like a kid on a coin-op airplane ride.

They saw him leap into a cloud of burning vapor just before the jet smashed into Dr. Destructo.

They fell silent as a mushroom cloud consumed the volcano and darkened the sun.

They cheered when Nightingale emerged from the flames and smoke, cradling Mantastic in her arms.

They rejoiced when Replay and Hairstrike burst out of the earth, leading the rest of the Fearless Five and a crowd of grateful heroes and villains to safety.

The world saw it all. But they didn't see me.

They didn't see Hugh catch me in his gigantic hand as he leaped from the jet.

They didn't see us fall through toxic smoke and fire and plunge into the sea.

Hugh wanted to stay with me, but I couldn't let him. The world needed to see Hugh-Mongous with his team.

They didn't need to see me.

So here I am. Drifting on the far side of the island. Looking up at the sky. At fumes and embers. At the island's desolation. And something else.

High in the column of ash, almost too far away to see, Destructo's silhouette. Making his escape.

The world doesn't see him. But I do.

What was this about? Why destroy the island? Why try to kill Mantastic? Was Destructo just doing what villains do? Or was it something else? Something more?

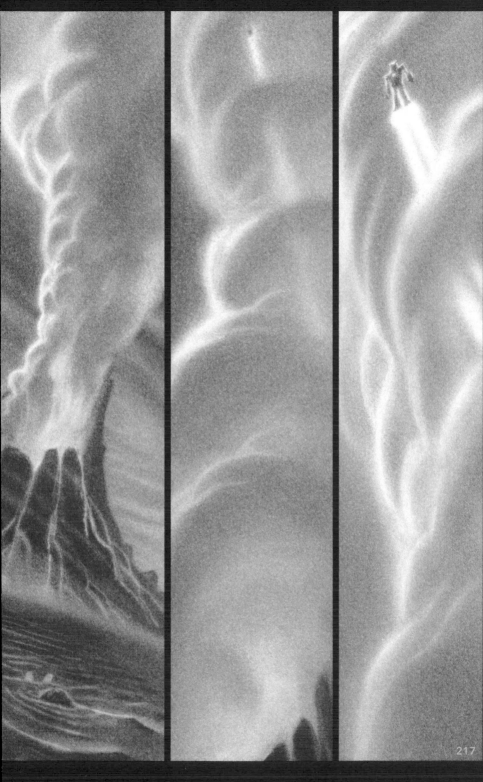

On the other side of the island, my friends were swarmed by reporters and grateful heroes. Even some of the villains took a time-out to thank them. The whole world was watching, and everyone wanted to know:

Who is this amazing new super-team?

My friends didn't have an answer. Everything had happened so fast, we hadn't discussed a team name. But the world needed an answer, so Arturo stepped up to the cameras, shot Mantastic a mocking smile, and said:

"They call us the Z-Team."

And just like that, a world-famous super-team was born!

The next morning at the breakfast table, Joy can't keep her freaky eyes off me. I pretend not to notice.

"The Z-Team." Electricity arcs from Dad's fingers, turning the bagel on Joy's plate a perfect, toasty brown. "Cool name. What's the 'Z' stand for?"

"I don't know. Does it have to stand for something?" Before I finish my sentence, I realize I just walked into one of Dad's hero-teaching traps.

"Of course! They're heroes. Heroes always stand for something. Need a warm-up, hon?"

"Sure, thanks." Mom's coffee cup looks tiny in her hand because she's twice as big as normal. She's towering over me as I scroll through an endless stream of Z-Team images and videos on my phone.

"I can't believe your friends saved the Fearless Five. I suppose I don't need to worry about you so much when you're with them."

I want to laugh. If Mom had any idea what's really going on, she'd lock me in my bunker for life. Instead, I just scored more freedom!

DING! A message pops onto my screen. I swipe it away but Mom's snooping powers are too fast. "What was that?"

"Huh? What?" I zoom into a pic of Ivy cradling Mantastic. "Mom, check this one out."

"Noah, that message said, 'Report to the Hall of Heroes ASAP.'"

Joy's eyes twinkle. She smells blood in the water. "Report to the Hall of Heroes? What does that mean?"

I'm sweating like a hot pig but try to play it cool. "What does that mean? Yeah, what *does* that mean? *Pfff*. That's funny."

Mom and Dad can't decide if I'm clueless or lying. Joy is loving the show.

I try again. "Oh, right! I totally forgot. . . . Yeah. . . . Arturo is . . . doing a report . . . on the Hall of Heroes. And he wants my help ASAP. So anyway, I'd better go. . . ."

I push back my chair, but Dad blocks my exit with a frying pan full of eggs. "Hold on. Have some breakfast first."

Joy mind-pulls me back against the table so tight I can barely breathe. "Yeah, have some breakfast first. Hey, Dad, you know all about the Hall of Heroes, right?"

"Sure do!" he says as he scoops a pile of eggs onto my plate. "I'm a bit of a Hall of Heroes expert. I'd be happy to help Arturo with his report."

Joy grins at me with half-lidded eyes. It's like a never-ending chess game with her!

I answer Dad through a mouthful of eggs. "Umm, okay, maybe."

"Invite him over," Dad says. "I'll toss on more eggs."

Now it's my move! I smile at Joy. "Sounds great. I'll text him."

I type a message into my phone, but not to Arturo:

hey grandma, need help w/ homework. M and D not home. wanna come over?

Joy's move. She floats a second helping of eggs onto my plate. "Grandma had fun with your new friends yesterday."

A laugh squeaks out of my nose along with some eggs. The thought of the Muscles getting their butts handed to them at the Old Oaks Home is too much to contain.

Mom's confused and a little grossed out. "What new friends? And what's so funny?"

"Oh, you know, just some friends from school . . . who like playing with old people. Cards and backgammon and stuff."

BZZZZZ–I glance under the table at my phone:

 OMW pumpkin. Be safe! :)

Joy counters, "Oh, and I found the fancy new helmet in your closet."

That little sneak! Why can't she stay out of my room?

"I tried it on but it got stuck. So I broke it."

Dad's curious. "Fancy new helmet?"

But Joy isn't done. "And I took apart your shiny suit. And that weird floating chair."

Mom looks at me. "Shiny suit? Floating chair? What's she talking about?"

I'm officially out of fake answers. "Uhhh . . ."

DING-DONG. The doorbell!

"I'll get it! I invited Grandma for breakfast."

Mom jumps up. "WHAT? Why would you? No! *I'll* get it."

Seconds later, Mom and Dad are battling seven Grandma hydra heads in the entryway.

Checkmate! I give Joy a victory smile and bolt for the back door. I turn the knob but the door won't budge. Joy is holding it shut with her mind!

"Joy, let go!"

WHAM! The door smacks me in the forehead! Owwww. I shake it off and rush across the backyard.

Replay and the team are waiting for me in that triangular spaceship from Asteroids. I hop inside and we blast off!

They're talking a mile a minute. *"This is unreal!" "We're famous!" "Did you see the number of likes and hearts?" "We have fans! Fans!"*

As we fly across the city, people everywhere point and wave. Some are even chanting, *"Z-Team! Z-Team! Z-Team!"*

Arturo takes a hard right, then a left, making a giant Z in the sky. The city cheers!

We round the back of Half Dome and land on the steps of the Hall of Heroes. My friends are in awe. Stunned, really. They're having the moment I had. But this one's a thousand times better because we're all together.

It's funny how big, important places make you want to be really, really quiet. We practically tiptoe through the front doors. The squeaking of our shoes, the swooshing of our pants—every little sound echoes off the columns and statues like the room wants us to know how enormous it is.

Ivy whispers to Tabitha, "Is this really our life now?"

Tabitha whispers back, "Maybe we'll have our own statues someday."

"MAYBE NOT! . . . *NOT* . . . *NOT* . . ."

We all jump back. Möbius's voice shakes the air. His giant, furious head materializes above us like the great and powerful Oz.

CHAPTER 15
Power Play

"NOAH! . . . *NOAH . . . NOAH . . .*
YOU DISREGARDED THE PLAN!"

"You arrogantly, foolishly, totally disregarded the plan!" Mantastic lands on Möbius's left, followed by the rest of the Fearless Five (assuming Rat is there). It's like standing in front of a judge and jury.

"BECAUSE OF YOUR REBELLION, THE MISSION WAS A COMPLETE AND UTTER FAILURE!"

Is he serious? "You call that a *failure*?"

Mantastic paces in front of us like a lawyer in stretchy pants. "You wasted the perfect opportunity to put Dr. Brain-Man and the Muscles on the map." He turns to my friends. "Sorry, kids, but you're done here."

Ivy steps forward. "Mr. Mantastic, Noah saved your life. And he did it with us, his team. We're not leaving him."

"If you want to get technical, Ivy, you saved my life," says Mantastic. "All Noah did was demolish our jet. This isn't up for discussion. Magic, please show the Z-Team the exit."

Unicorn Magic waves a hoof. "Let's hang out some-time. Noah has my number." A swirl of sparkly dust lifts my friends off the ground and carries them toward the door.

"Magic, wait!" I say. "Please! Hold on!" She pauses my friends in midair.

I plead my case. "Your honor . . . Dang, I mean Professor, respectfully, you're wrong. The mission was a success! Have you seen what's going on out there? The world loves the Z-Team. Arturo, show 'em!"

Arturo fills the room with screens displaying Z-Team memes and looping video clips. Mantastic ignores them. "Nice try, bro, but—"

I continue, "The mission objective was to put a new super-team on the map. Not only did the Z-Team defeat Dr. Destructo, they saved the Fearless Five. Everyone is talking about them." I point to the photo of Nightingale cradling Mantastic. "This image has been shared, like, TWENTY MILLION TIMES!"

Spider Monkey laughs. "I shared it fifty times myself!" Monkey pats Mantastic on the shoulder. "Sorry, man, it's just too good."

Rat is laughing too. "I sent it to my entire Rat Pack o' Rat Fans!"

Mantastic's eyes glow rage-red.

Möbius is silent. It's hard to know what he's thinking behind those granny glasses. Mantastic is less mysterious.

"Ha. Ha. Ha. Go ahead," he says. "Get it out of your systems 'cause that's the last time you're gonna see me cradled like a baby. Nobody, I repeat, *nobody* cradles Mantastic!"

His words loop in my mind. "Nobody cradles Mantastic."

Inspiration strikes! "That's it!" I shout. "We have to do that again!"

Mantastic ignores me. "Magic, will you please get these kids—"

I run to one of the screens. "No, don't you see! The Z-Team needs to save the Fearless Five again. And again and again and again! Think about it—what better way to show the world the Z-Team deserves to be number one than to have the Z-Team rescue the #1 Hero Team?"

Arturo smirks at Mantastic. "Again and again and again."

Mantastic burns. "Not a chance! I've never thrown a fight in my life. Giving up the number one spot is one thing, but I'm not gonna be fake-saved by these . . . these . . ."

"Kid's got a point," Monkey says. "And I'd pay to see more Baby-tastic pictures. No offense, dude."

Sweet! They're catching the vision. "And may I point out, I have a much better shot at staying alive if I'm not fighting actual super-villains all day long."

Mindstorm speaks to our brains, *«And I can use the mind link to keep Noah connected to the Z-Team from a safe distance.»*

Hugh giggles. "It tickles so much!"

"Great idea, Mindstorm! Keeping me alive is definitely in the plus column."

"Hold on," Mantastic says. "Aren't you forgetting something, baby Einstein? How are we supposed to get you near the Super Stone if you aren't part of the Z-Team?"

Unicorn Magic lights up like a Christmas tree. "Ooooh, I have an idea. Leave that to me."

Mantastic turns to Möbius. "We aren't really doing this?"

Möbius is motionless. Is he thinking? Sleeping? Dead?

"YES! . . . *YES* . . . *YES* . . ." Everyone jumps! Dang, he's loud.

"YES, WE ARE REALLY DOING THIS. MANTASTIC, YOU KNOW THE MISSION IS MORE IMPORTANT THAN ANY ONE OF US, AND THAT BEING A HERO OFTEN REQUIRES SACRIFICE."

Mantastic's jaw tenses. I think he's fighting a super-battle with his pride. He takes a deep breath and somehow stands up even straighter, then nods.

Möbius booms, "THE PLAN IS HEREBY REVISED: THE Z-TEAM WILL SHOW THE WORLD THEY DESERVE TO BE THE #1 HERO TEAM BY RESCU- ING THE FEARLESS FIVE AGAIN AND AGAIN AND AGAIN . . . *AND AGAIN* . . . *AND AGAIN* . . ."

Magic punctuates the moment by filling the room with rainbows and tiny glowing ponies.

Arturo can't resist. "Oh yeah! It's time to play a little *SAVE MANTASTIC!*"

Mantastic blasts him through the wall.

The next few weeks are a blur as the Z-Team fake-rescues the Fearless Five from all sorts of perilous predicaments. But that's not all—we're also taking on big-time villains! I'm able to coach from the shadows, which keeps me safe, and because I don't suffer from super-brain, we have an edge. I give solutions the villains don't expect, like why fight a fire titan if you can trick him into chasing you into the ocean?

The Z-Team is climbing the hero charts at record speed. And not just in the Super States. We have Z-Fans all over the world! Every other day, we take a quick, suborbital ride on the new Justice Jet for an international mission. So cool! Every time it's Replay's turn to save Mantastic, he marks it on his digital world map.

But I've gotta say, it's hard watching the Five throw so many battles, pretending to be less than they are. I think it physically pains Mantastic every time he has to thank my friends in front of news cameras.

But the plan is working. Everywhere we go, we see more Z-Team fans. There's something about my friends that inspires people. Maybe because they aren't your typical hero team. They aren't like the Muscles. They're more like all the other people. The quirky ones, the quiet ones, the little ones—the Z-people in the world. Those are the ones wearing Z T-shirts and putting Z pins on their backpacks.

Oh and check this—Hugh has an action figure that shouts, "GOOOO BIIIIG!" Tabitha has a line of hair products and quirky fashion accessories. Arturo has a video game called Replay's Reboot. And wait for it. . . . The Z-Team has its own comic book! Issue #1 has Nightingale saving Mantastic on the cover, so now Ivy has a million dedicated fanboys. Not cool.

We've been on marketing and mission overload, so when we're

not running on adrenaline, we're dead tired. My parents think I'm just working really hard at school. That's because Möbius is pulling strings behind the scenes to make it look like I'm living my normal life. I think Joy might know more than she's letting on 'cause she's hardly said a word to me in weeks, and I catch her watching me all the time.

This morning when I told Mom and Dad I was headed to school it was actually true. Möbius says it's good marketing for the Z-Team to be seen living their "everyday lives." Apparently fans love that stuff. He also said to expect a surprise. Whatever that means.

I hop, skip, duck, and tumble my way across town like I've done hundreds of times before. My friends land around me just like normal.

But a few seconds later, nothing is normal.

Maybe ever again.

CHAPTER 16

Pride Goeth . . .

We walk onto campus in what feels like slow motion. The entire school is watching us with wide eyes. Well, not me, but my friends. Suddenly the quad is a selfie fest. Everyone wants a picture with the Z-Team. I'm squeezed out into the crowd, where I hear things like:

"I have fifth period with Arturo."

"Hugh went to my preschool."

"Tabitha is my bestie!" FYI, Tabitha has NO IDEA who that girl is.

My neighbor elbows me. "Dude, Ivy lives on my block and she's totally got a crush on me." Hello, I live on your block. And no, she doesn't.

It's weird. I'm part of the team, but right now it doesn't feel like it because their job is to be seen, and mine is to be unseen. It's got me thinking about stuff my dad says. You know, about what being a real hero is all about.

Suddenly the theme music from the Z-Team animated series plays over the school's PA system. Then Professor Möbius's voice thunders:

"CONGRATULATIONS TO HALF DOME BAY'S VERY OWN Z-TEAM—THE WORLD'S NEW #1 HERO TEAM!"

What? We did it?

The school goes wild! Students, teachers, janitors—everyone blasts their powers into the air like fireworks!

My friends are mobbed by adoring fans. I'm so happy for them, and proud. But the moment stings a little. This should be my celebration too. I'm even sort of their leader. Part of me wishes I wasn't here, until Ivy pushes her way through the crowd and throws her arms around me.

"We did it, Noah! We did it!"

Never mind. BEST. DAY. EVER.

Hugh, Arturo, and Tabitha dog-pile us. My pity party is officially over. "Okay, Z-Team, give 'em what they want."

My friends switch into their super-suits and blast off for a victory lap above the school. I'm grounded near the lockers, but it feels like I'm up there with them.

SNAP!

Too bad I'm not. Something wraps around my ankle and hoists me into the air! I'm hanging upside down by Catfight's tail, surrounded by the Muscles!

Maximus cracks his neck. "Grandma's not here to save you this time, punk! That should have been us! The Magnificent Muscles shoulda been the #1 Hero Team!"

Hit-Man slams his gloves together in my face. "You chose the wrong team, buttsqueak. You coulda been a Muscle! But you gave it aaaall up. Now look at you. Your freaky friends are number one and yer nobody!"

But he's wrong. I am somebody. I'm the genius leader of the world's #1 Hero Team, which means I can take these gym rats.

The Muscles flex and wind up for a beatdown. I scan my surroundings—hallway, lockers, quad. . . . *The QUAD.* It's packed with amped-up heroes just itching for villains to pound!

Maximus gives the prefight one-liner: "All aboard the pain train—"

"WHAT?!" I shout as loud as I can.

The Muscles freeze. Maximus clears his throat. "I said, all aboard—"

"NO WAY!" I yell. "You guys are UNDERCOVER VILLAINS?!"

Behind the Muscles, a hundred hero heads whip around.

Maximus is confused. "What? I didn't say that. I said, 'All aboard the—'"

"AND your REAL NAME is the MUSCLES OF MAYHEM?!"

More and more heroes are tuning in, unbuttoning shirts, pulling masks on over their heads.

Catfight clarifies, "Norman, that's not what he said—"

"WHAT?!" I keep going. "You think heroes are SHRIMP NUGGET WUSSY BABIES and you can SQUASH 'EM ALL with your SUPER-SWOLE BICEPS?"

Before the Muscles can say another word, they're mobbed by super-brain-crazed heroes! "Defeat the Muscles of Mayhem!" "NO VILLAINS ALLOWED!"

Half the school stampedes past me for some villain-pounding fun. Mission accomplished!

I take in the whole glorious scene: My friends having the time of their lives. The Muscles fleeing like baby chickens. And me, the cool, mysterious, unknown hero leader, making it all happen.

My phone BUZZES with a message. . . .

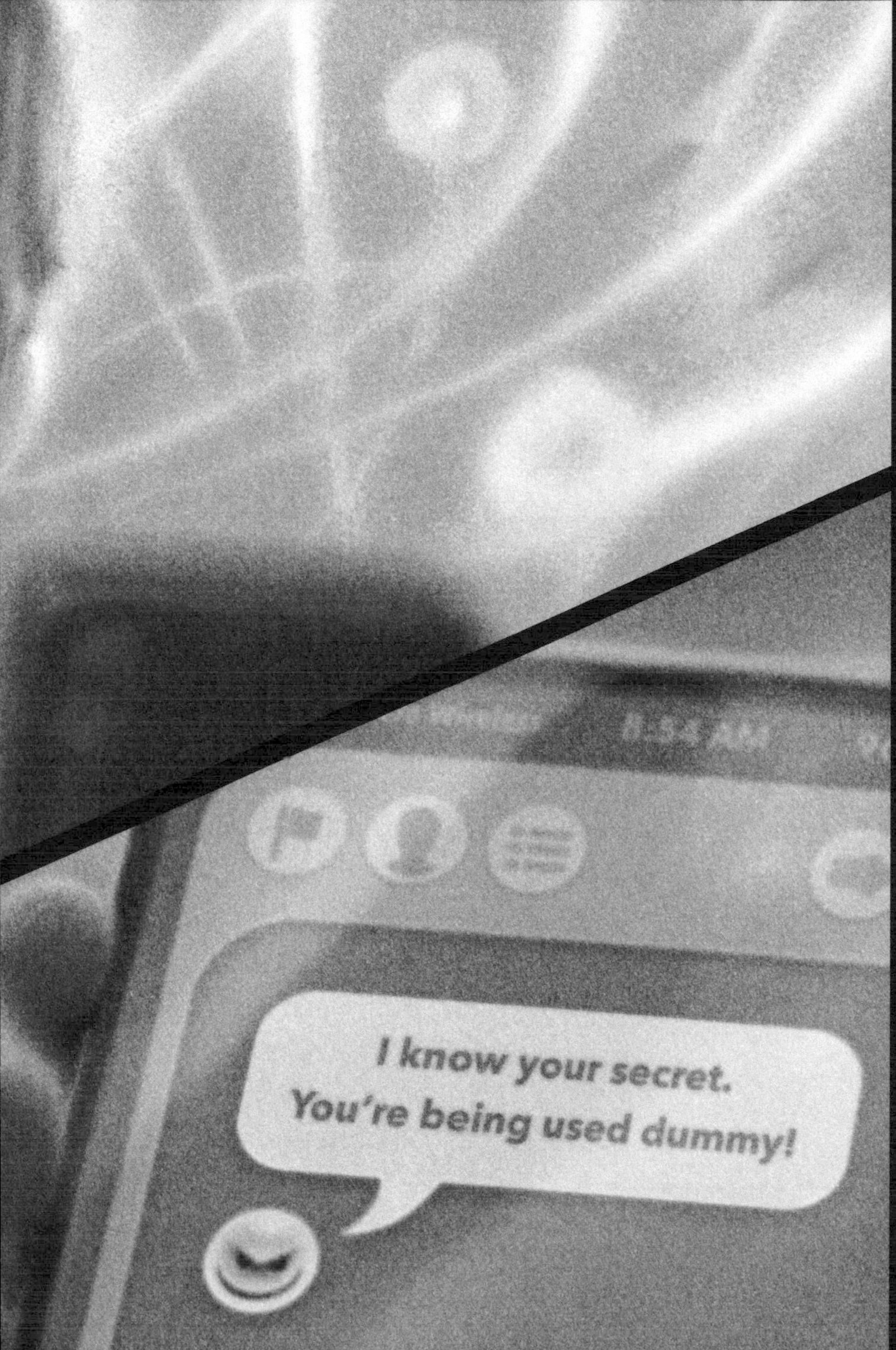
I know your secret.
You're being used dummy!

CHAPTER 17
Friends and Frenemies

USED? And WHO knows?! I check the sender's name: Nunn O. Yerbizness.

Is this a joke? I hope it's a joke.

I've gotta talk to Möbius right away. I need somewhere private, so I bolt for the library. I'm on autopilot, bobbing and weaving around heroes and stray blasts. The message loops in my mind. It's probably a wrong number. Or super-spam. Yeah, probably nothing. But what if it isn't?

I duck inside the library. Nobody's here. Bookworm must be out celebrating too. I slip into the History aisle and pull out my phone.

It's dead. Not no-service dead, but *black-screen dead*!

The lights go out! The library is pitch-black. I hear the clock ticking on the wall, and the muffled war zone celebration outside. Then something else. Down the aisle, in the blackness . . . a *whirring*, like tiny gears.

"Hello-o-o-o-oo?" My voice cracks; my hands are shaking. "Mr. Almaraz, is that you? Bookworm?"

I squint hard, I can barely see. . . . A *toy* . . . A Dr. Destructo toy. It's marching toward me, then stops.

"Hello? Is someone there?" The little Destructo eyes flicker red, then flash! Rays of light stream out, forming a huge hologram of Dr. Destructo!

247

I'm startled back against the shelf. Encyclopedias
bounce off my head as I slide to the floor.

"Bwwwah-hahahaha!" Hologram-Destructo towers
over me. My whole body is shaking.

His maniacal laugh settles into a chuckle. "Sorry,
kiddo. Didn't mean to scare ya. Villain habit."

He taps a button on his wrist panel. Pharrell's "Happy"
plays through his suit speakers.

"Noah, I'm not here to hurt you. I'm here to *enlighten*
you! Ya see, anyone with a head . . . Whoa, whoa, whoa,

time out. Wrong mood music. Just a sec. . . ."

Anyone with a head?

He scrolls through a playlist on his wrist display. "Nope, nope, too techno, too country. . . . Anyhoo, where were we? Oh yeah, the head thing. Ya see, Noah, anyone with a head on his shoulders, which is basically Professor Möbius and me—though that weirdo doesn't have shoulders—knows that you are the world's *most powerful weapon*. Unfortunately, he got to you first. So I'm here to do a little un-brainwashing."

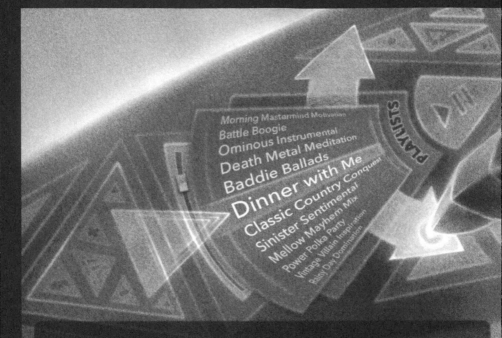

Morning Mastermind Motivation
Battle Boogie
Ominous Instrumental
Death Metal Meditation
Baddie Ballads
Dinner with Me
Classic Country Conquest
Sinister Sentimental
Mellow Mayhem Mix
Power Polka Party
Vintage Villain Inspiration
Rainy Day Domination

PLAYLISTS

What's he talking about? Doesn't matter. Just stay cool.

"Ah! Here we go!" He taps a button.

Sentimental piano music fills the library. "Noah, you and I are kindred, simpatico, like two peas in a pod, peanut butter and jelly, mac and cheese."

"More like orange juice and toothpaste."

"Ha! Claaaaassic Noah line!" He shakes his head like we're old pals. "But for realzees, we're more alike than you think. You wouldn't guess it, but I have a soft spot for you in my titanium-plated heart." *Klink-klink-klink.* He taps his chest insignia with his claw.

"You see, boss, in the Old World, I was a pathetic nobody just like you. For serious! Nobody knew my name. Sound familiar?"

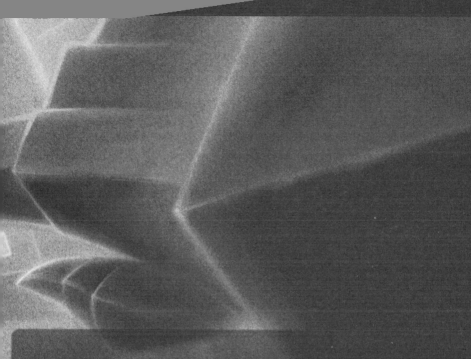

He's probably lying. But even if he's not, I won't get sucked in.

Destructo skips to a new track. The music starts soft, then builds from one inspiring movement to another as he jabbers on. "But did I care if the world ignored me? Nope! Because, just like you, I knew I was meant for more. That I was destined for greatness!"

He turns like he's gazing at something a jillion miles away, slowly reaching out his claw. "That somehow, someday, I'd be the ultimate somebody! So when the meteorite struck, I knew it was meant for me!" *KLANG!* He smacks his chest and turns back to me, as if I care.

"And check it—I was totally right! Look at me now. Half the world loves me, and the other half looooves to hate me! But guess what? They ALL know my name!"

I shake my head. "You wanna destroy the world just so people will know your name? That's pathetic."

"Destroy the world? Kid, I'm trying to save it!"

Okay, now he's just talking full-blown nonsense. "You think I'm an idiot? I'm supposed to believe that a guy named *DESTRUCTO* wants to *SAVE* the world?"

"Come on, Noah. You're smart enough to see that my awesomely ironic villain name is the perfect cover for my real plan. Just like how heroes babble on about 'saving' the world when really—"

"The heroes *are* saving the world!" I shout over him. "From villains like you!"

Destructo shakes his head, "Wow, they've done it. They've got you talking just like them. Come on, buddy, you know better than that—the 'heroes' aren't trying to save anything."

"You're wrong!"

"Am I?" He taps a button on his wrist. *BUM-BU-BUM-BUMM* . . . Deep, ominous music rattles the air. "Tell me, Noah, who turned the Great Wall into the Short Fence last week to defeat Dragantor and his Serpent Samurais?"

"How should I know?"

"It was Panda-Monium. A hero. And who dropped Mighty Mount Everest into the Grand Power-Canyon last night to vanquish the Tombstone Terror Titans?"

"Mount Everest is gone? And the Grand Canyon?!"

"Gone forever. But that's okay, right? Since the Power Princesses reached number 923 on the hero charts."

Destructo's hologram grows, filling the aisle. Books topple; his eyes burn. "And who melted the Super-Statue of Liberty? Who demolished the Pyramids? Who destroyed Powerdise Island?

"What?! Powerdise Island? *You* did!"

"No, *you* did, Noah. You destroyed Powerdise Island just to keep me from building a vacation fortress. But it was worth it, right? Because you and your friends got to play hero in front of the whole world."

BUM-BUM-BUMMMM! The music climaxes, then dies, leaving my heartbeat pounding in my ears. My head is swimming. I don't know what to think. Is he right?

Destructo relaxes and lets the moment sink in. "Come on, pal, there are no heroes or villains. It's all a game. You used to know that. But every day, the game gets more catastrophic. If we don't stop it now, it'll be *GAME OVER* for everyone."

"But we *are* stopping it!"

Destructo laughs. "Sure you are—you and Professor Boobius have a plan, right?"

Dang it! I said too much.

"Here's the thing, muchacho: Professor No-body is a liar-liar-no-pants-on-fire. That's right! And the smartest kind of liar-liar-no-pants-on-fire because his lies are hidden in what he *doesn't* tell you."

I think he's trying to get me to talk. I won't take the bait.

"Professor Head Games is holding out on you—he hasn't told you the all-important second half of his secret plan to 'save' the world."

He's gotta be bluffing. Now it's my turn. "There is *NO* secret plan!"

"Okay, Amateur Hour. Try this on for size." He clears his throat. "*During the ceremony to crown the #1 Hero Team, No-Power Noah will sneak into the Power Dome, secure the leaking Super Stone, and hand it over to Professor Bobblehead.* How am I doing so far?"

"Wait, how do you know—?"

"Please, I'm an evil genius. I know things. Tell me, little man, has Professor Flöatius told you what he plans to do with the Stone once he's got it?"

"He's gonna secure it."

"'*Secure it*'? HA! Okay, sure. He'll 'secure it.' Then what?"

"Then nothing. The Stone won't leak anymore, and the world will be safe."

"Safe? Noah, you've been around awhile. Tell me, what happens when heroes get *more* power? Is it safe? Do you feel *safe*?"

"What are you talking about?"

"It seems the 'good' professor forgot to mention

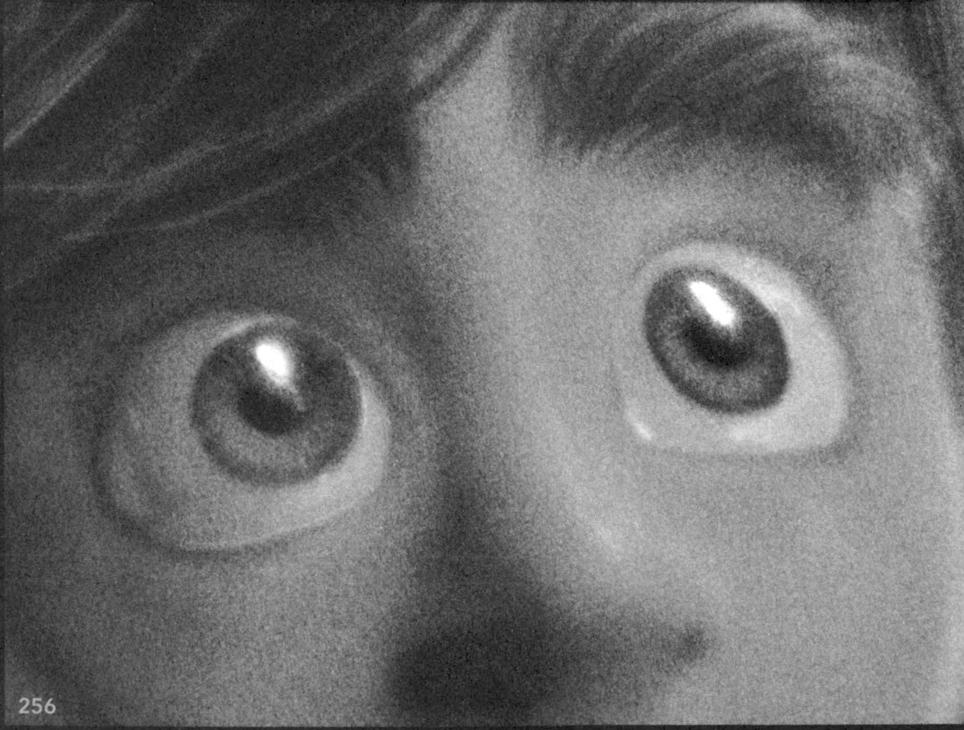

how he plans to use the Stone to give MORE POWER to *every hero on the planet!*"

I scramble to my feet. "What? More power?! No, that's not the plan! He wouldn't. . . . I mean . . . the world wouldn't last—"

"A week! The world wouldn't last a week! See, Noah? You get it! Mac and cheese! Told you we're on the same page. Which is why you're going to give the Super Stone to ME instead."

"Give the Stone to you? Are you insane?'"

"Sure, a little bit. I mean, I do want to rule the world. But I don't want to destroy it. I want to save it *so I can rule it*. See how that works?"

My mind races, sifting through everything he said, trying to catch him in a lie—he has to be lying. Does Möbius really want to—?

"Think about it, Noah. Would you rather have one super-cool, all-powerful villain establish world order? Or let three billion all-powerful do-gooders crack the planet in half?"

I can barely breathe. My whole body feels tight.

"Hey, I know I'm dropping a brain-busting, double-bacon bombshell on you right now, so let me make it easy. Either do the right thing and give me the Stone, or I'll make your sister my number two."

"What? Joy?!" A surge of energy shoots through me! I lock eyes with the villain.

"You may be the world's most dangerous weapon, but Joy comes in a close second. That's right, I know about her dual powers. Quite a family ya got there, kiddo!"

Every muscle in my body tenses rock hard. I've never wanted power as much as I do right now!

"Leave . . . her . . . alone!"

"Leave *her* alone? Ha! More like leave *me* alone. She sends me fan mail every day." His wrist DINGS with a notification. "Oh look, she just liked my post. Hold on, lemme heart that. . . ."

He taps his wrist—*BLING*—then looks back at me like everything's fine, like I don't want to crunch him like a tin can.

"Don't worry, Noah, once you give me the Stone, you and your family will never see me again. Unless you wanna hang out or whatever. I think you'd like me if you got to know me."

I glare at him, hard as stone. His words die in the air between us.

"Oookey-dokey . . . So we're cool? Cool. You've had a big day, so that's all for now. Chat soon, partner!"

He clicks a button. The projection ends.

The library lights flicker on.

WHAT JUST HAPPENED?!

My legs wobble. I fall back against the shelves.

Destructo has to be lying about Möbius. Right? Möbius wouldn't really power up all the heroes . . . *would he?*

I need answers!

I rush out of the library into clouds of dust and smoke.

The quad is smolder-ing and empty. The Z-Team celebration has moved into the city, leaving the school completely destroyed.

By villains? No, by heroes.

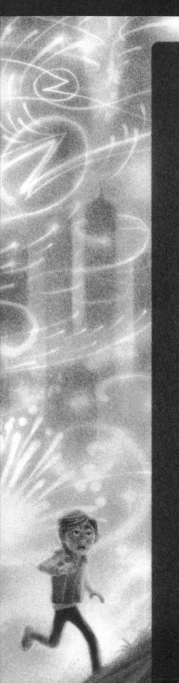

CHAPTER 18

Missions Impossible

A cataclysmic celebration rips through the city like a forest fire as news spreads of the Z-Team hitting number one.

Just the thought of these people getting more power . . . I have to get to the Hall of Heroes to talk to Möbius!

On the bright side, no one cares about "saving" me right now, so I'm moving fast, avoiding as much friendly fire as possible, and I arrive at the Hall of Heroes with only a few bruises and a minor chemical burn. I sprint up the steps and through the entrance. The lights are low; it seems empty.

"Helloooooo? Anybody here? Professor?" My voice echoes. This place could really use a receptionist.

"NOAH. . . . *NOAH . . . NOAH . . .* I'M IN THE SITUATION ROOM. . . . *ROOM . . . ROOM . . .*"

I head toward Möbius's voice. The doors to the situation room are open, but it's pitch-black inside. What's going on? I step into the darkness.

"Professor, I need to ask you—"

FLASH! The room EXPLODES . . .

. . . with confetti, glitter, and tiny, magical dancing kittens wearing party hats.

"SURPRISE!"

What's going on? Everybody's here. Unicorn Magic swooshes a hat onto my head as Arturo and Hugh mummify me with silly string.

Spider Monkey high-fives me with all four hands. "This is *your* day too, man! We just had to keep your congrats on the down low."

Everyone sings about how I'm a "jolly good fellow" as they slap me on the back and ruffle my hair.

Okay, this is the coolest. And I want to enjoy it, but my mind is a hamster wheel of fear and doubt. I squeeze through the group to get to Möbius.

"Professor, can we talk?"

Möbius stops singing. "GENIUS IDEA, NOAH. LET'S TALK!"

Everyone listens.

"LET'S TALK ABOUT . . . CAKE! . . . *CAKE . . . CAKE . . .*"

Cheers all around as a gigantic cake descends from the ceiling.

Tabitha attacks it with her knife-wielding hair tentacles. She's like a team of Benihana chefs—slicing, dicing, plating. Spider Monkey is a whirlwind of hands and feet as he passes out plates, forks, and napkins.

Arturo shouts, "Speeeech!"

Everyone joins in. "SPEECH, SPEECH, SPEECH!"

They're all looking at me—Ivy, my friends, the Five, the kittens. It feels pretty great.

"Umm, wow, I didn't expect this, you guys. I mean, thanks, and . . . I don't know what to say."

"NOAH, IN ANY OTHER SITUATION, HUMILITY WOULD BE ENTIRELY APPROPRIATE, GIVEN YOUR INSUFFICIENCIES. BUT TODAY IS DIFFERENT, FOR YOUR WEAKNESS HAS MADE US STRONG! AND SOON, EVEN STRONGER! SPEECH! SPEECH! SPEECH!"

Suddenly, Destructo's words flood my mind— *"His lies are hidden in what he doesn't tell you. . . . There are no heroes or villains. It's all a game. . . . If we don't stop it now, it'll be GAME OVER for everyone!"*

My brain clicks back online.

"Professor, what will you do with the Super Stone once you have it?"

"Weird speech, man," Rat says from somewhere.

Möbius booms, "AH, YES, THAT WAS MEANT TO BE A SURPRISE! BUT NOW SEEMS THE PERFECT OCCASION TO REVEAL THE MOST GENIUS PART OF MY GENIUS PLAN TO SAVE THE WORLD!"

The room is breathless with anticipation, all eyes locked on Möbius.

"AS SOON AS THE SUPER STONE'S POWER IS SAFELY CONTAINED IN THE CONTROLLER, I WILL USE IT TO GIVE *DOUBLE* POWER . . . NAY! *TRIPLE* POWER . . . NAY! *NEAR-INFINITE* POWER TO EVERY HERO ON THE PLANET! VILLAINS WILL NEVER, EVER WIN, EVER AGAIN, *EVER!*"

The room erupts with cheers, chest bumps, blasts, sparkles . . . *"I'll be as big as a mountain!" "I'll fly faster than light!" "I'll wrap the whole planet with hair!"*

This is a nightmare. Destructo was right!

"Whoa, whoa, whoa!" I shout. "The last thing you guys need is MORE power!"

They freeze in mid-celebration.

"NOAH, NOAH. YOU DEAR, TENDER SNOWFLAKE OF A HERO. IT IS TRUE WE WILL BE EVEN MORE POWERFUL, WHILE YOU WILL REMAIN FEEBLE AND WEIRD. BUT YOU MUSTN'T LET JEALOUSY BEFUDDLE YOUR FRAGILE BRAIN—THOUGH THERE IS CERTAINLY SO, SO MUCH TO BE JEALOUS OF."

"Jealous? I'm not jealous! And I'm definitely not the one with a befuddled brain!"

"Duuude," says Rat, "you're totally poopin' the party."

"I don't care about the party! Have you seen what's going on out there?! Heroes are trashing everything! There's hardly anything left of the Old World—*MY world*—and nobody cares! All you care about is POWER!"

Awkward silence.

Then Möbius glides closer, lowering his eyes to my level. "NOAH, PLEASE FORGIVE ME. I AM SO SORRY."

My shoulders relax.

"BUT I HAVE NO IDEA WHAT YOU ARE TALKING ABOUT." His giant brow furrows. "THOUGH CLEARLY YOU WANT THE *VILLAINS TO WIN*!"

"What?! NO! I don't want *anyone* to *WIN*! You're the one who told me this isn't a game, but you're the one acting like it is!"

"Listen, everybody," says Mantastic. "Noah's right."

Wow, I didn't expect him to take my side.

"This IS like a game! A game we're going to win! Over and over and over!"

Monkey and Rat join in. *"And over and over and over . . . ,"* followed by Hugh and Tabitha, *"and over and over . . ."*

There's nothing I can do. They're all sick. They hear me, but they can't understand. They'll never understand.

Magic throws her arms around me. "Oh, Noah, just

think how safe you'll be in a world full of extra-super-duper-heroes!"

Möbius's voice booms over the chants and cheers. "TOMORROW OUR HERO DREAMS BEGIN! WE LEAVE FOR POWER PARK IN THE MORNING!"

More confetti . . . and music . . . and kittens.

Hugh starts a new chant: *"Power Park! Power Park! Power Park!"*

I want to scream, but I hold it in. Anything I do or say will just make them worse.

I need to get away, to be alone. I toss my cake and hat into the trash and head out the door. Nobody notices. How could they? They're super-crazed.

Whenever stuff really gets to me, I come up to Glacier Point. The quiet, the breeze, the solitude. It helps me regroup and reset.

I try to push everything out of my mind. But today it pushes back: What have I done? What do I do now? Why am I even here? Is there any hope left for me? For my friends? My family? My world?

The sky is yellow and pink. The edges of the clouds burn like fire as the sun goes down.

In the Old World, my parents were totally into sunsets. No matter what we were doing, Dad made us stop for "sunset appreciation." But they don't notice things like this anymore. Nobody does.

Why couldn't that stupid meteorite have picked some other planet?

A flash catches my eye from the top of Half Dome— a ray of sunlight reflecting off the Justice Jet. They're prepping it for tomorrow's trip.

Ugh. Tomorrow's trip. I wish I could hide up here forever, but I can't. Somehow I have to choose between two impossible plans:

1. Destructo's plan, where a villain RULES the world.

OR

2. Möbius's plan, where heroes DESTROY the world.

I watch the clouds, wishing an answer would come from above. They roll and drift, like a river flowing across the sky. Sunlight flashes . . . streams through . . . stings my eyes. The sun is so powerful.

The thought parks at the front of my mind: The sun is so powerful.

What did Möbius say when he kidnapped me?

"IT WOULD TAKE THE FUSION POWER OF A STAR TO DESTROY THE SUPER STONE."

Wait . . . a *star*? That's it! The sun!

I jump to my feet. Sunlight bathes my body with warmth and *hope*.

Forget plans 1 and 2, I'm going with:

3. Noah's plan, where I SAVE the world!

I bolt across the city, navigating my way through the normal obstacle course of absurdity. I jump, duck, pivot, hop-hop-hop, hit the deck, roll-roll-roll, speed crawl, scan left-right-left. . . .

Time passes but I don't feel it. I only feel motion . . . energy . . . and purpose. I'm almost home.

I rush through the front door and into the kitchen. I riffle through the drawers. Nope. SLAM! Nope. SLAM! Shoot, where is it?!

"MOM, WHERE'S THE ALUMINUM FOIL?"

"We're out!" she shouts from the office. "Joy used it to make her mini Destructo-Troopers. Why? What do you need it for?"

"Nothing! Never mind!"

Crud! Where am I gonna—? Wait . . . IDEA!

I race upstairs to my closet. I yank the lid off the box in the corner and grab my Meteor Man costume.

I tear off a wide strip of foil, fold it, and stuff it into my backpack.

"GOING SOMEWHERE?" Mom's voice startles me!

I whip around. She's towering over me.

I'm out of breath but try to play it cool. "Who, me? Going somewhere? Umm . . ."

She shrinks to normal size. "Just kidding. You're going to Power Park tomorrow! Professor Möbius invited you to ride in the Justice Jet with the Z-Team. Wow, talk about an exciting first plane ride. I'm just happy you'll be in good hands!"

"Riiiiiight, *first* plane ride. And yep, totally good, totally safe hands."

Mom turns to go. "It'll be a day to remember!"

I zip my backpack shut. "You can say that again."

She stops at the door. "We'll meet you there."

"What?! I . . . I mean . . . *what* do you mean?"

Joy floats into the doorway with a tiny wheelie suitcase.

"You don't think we'd miss your friends' big day? And besides, your sister will love it."

Joy's mouth curls into a creepy grin. "Yeah, I can't wait."

CHAPTER 19

Power Trip

The Justice Jet rockets through the stratosphere like a chromium-plated shooting star, gleaming with ultra-high-tech grace and power. Inside, it's more like a school bus on its way to summer camp. Everyone is singing road-trip songs as we speed toward Power Park. Well, everyone but me. I have other things on my mind.

In order to hurl the Super Stone into the sun, I'm gonna need to "borrow" the Justice Jet, so I'm laser-focused on Spider Monkey in the pilot's seat. I've gotta memorize his every move. It doesn't help that he has four hands and loves fiddling with knobs and switches just for fun!

"Noah, you okay?" Ivy scoots in next to me.

"Huh? Yeah. Fine."

"You seem stressed."

"No, no, I'm cool." I pat my stomach. "You know me and planes."

It's not a complete lie; I am pretty queasy. I think she suspects it isn't the whole truth, but she gives me space.

Spider Monkey shouts, "Landing sequence initiated!" Landing sequence? Crud, I really needed to see that part!

We touch down at the edge of Power Park, the most colossal theme park the world has ever seen. The whole place is, you guessed it, super themed. Every land, ride, show, and snack is inspired by a famous hero or villain.

Power Park is one of the only places in Superworld where people prefer their secret identities over their super identities. They love being superhero fans, almost as much as they love being super them-selves. So there's kind of an unwritten rule—in Power Park, you can cosplay other heroes or villains, you just can't wear your own super-suit since that would ruin the fan fun. Which is why today, Power Park is filled with heroes and villains dressed in homemade Z-Team costumes.

Actually, the whole place is like a giant Z fest. They've got Z hats, balloons, pins, and even Z characters signing autographs. If the fans knew who we were, we'd be mobbed, so we're incognito, sporting "Smith Family Vacay" T-shirts and ridiculous hats.

Mantastic and Magic are posing as our parents, leading us down Mega Main Street. Their real names are Chet and Carla, which is totally weird. But not nearly as weird as seeing Carla without her unicorn head.

I'm busy scanning the park for the next part of my plan. In order to escape with the Super Stone, I'll have to give Destructo a fake one. This means I need to find a souvenir shop, then somehow ditch my friends for a while.

"Okay, *Smith family*." Carla links her arm through Chet's. "Let's go over the plan for tomorrow's big ceremony."

Chet isn't listening. He's fixated on the Replay park character posing for photos. The line of Replay fans stretches all the way to Urban Disaster Land. Chet searches the crowd in every direction, then shakes his head in disbelief. I think there's a tiny tear in his eye.

"This place used to be crawling with Mantastics."

Arturo points across the street. "Cheer up, *Dad*. There's tons of Mantastics over there."

We turn and see an "80% OFF" bargain bin overflowing with Mantastic toys. But something else catches my eye. . . .

In the shop window, between the toys, capes, masks, and helmets–a SOUVENIR SUPER STONE!

Meanwhile, Chet has Arturo in a headlock. "Boys, stop roughhousing!" says Carla as she rushes to separate them.

Now's my chance! I discreetly sidestep away from the group.

"Noah, my son!" Carla shouts. "We still have a job . . . I mean, *family fun* to do."

Dang it, I'll have to try again later.

Carla corrals the group, then launches into the plan to

sneak me inside the Power Dome. "The Z-Team parade will end right in front of the Dome. Then the crowning ceremony will begin. Noah, my darling boy, you'll be strategically stationed . . . umm . . . I mean, you will be *enjoying the parade* from the top of–"

"HA-HA-HA! Nice outfits! Y'all look like a box of Goobers!"

That's Destructo's voice! I spin around. . . . No one's there.

"BOO!"

"Aggghh!" I jump a foot in the air! I search left, right, up, down. . . . Where is he?!

"Sorry, partner." Destructo laughs. "I couldn't resist. I wired your hat. You're the only one who can hear me."

I feel Tabitha's hair around my shoulders. She spins me back toward the group. "You okay, little brother. Or *big* brother? Or *twin* brother? Or *uncle*–"

"Yeah, yeah, yeah. Totes. Anyway, Carla, you were saying?"

"Oh, *son of mine,* you are soooo funny. Always calling me–YOUR MOM–by my *first* name."

"Right, sorry . . . *Mom,* you were saying?"

Carla winks at me like we're super-spies and continues divulging key locations and assignments. Unfortunately, I'm not getting a word of it because Destructo's voice is rattling my skull through my hat.

"Blah, blah, blah . . . then Professor Dörkius will crown the new sucker-team. You'll slip inside the Dome through a secret hatch. Soooo original. Then, if you don't disintegrate, you'll pop the Stone into the controller and badda-bing-badda-boom! *Their* plan ends and *ours* begins: I'll meet you in the Dome, snatch the Stone, and—drumroll, please—RUUULE THE WOOORLD!"

Carla finishes, ". . . and SAAAVE THE WOOORLD!"

Hugh flexes his secret identity's nonexistent biceps. "Then it's time to *POWER UP! POWER UP!*"

Tabitha, Arturo, and Chet join in. *"POWER UP! POWER UP! POWER UP!"*

Destructo chuckles inside my hat. "Remember when you didn't believe these wing nuts were power hungry?"

My brain feels like a blender set to liquefy. Can this get any worse?

"NOAH!"

It's Mom! My actual mom. And Dad, and Joy, and Grandma. Ugh, four more. Now I have to lose TEN people!

Mom waves as they weave through the crowd toward us. "Congratulations, you guys! We're so excited. Tomorrow's your big day!"

Some nearby Z-Fans turn to listen.

Mom notices my shirt. "Who are the Smiths?"

I grab Carla's weird non-hoof hand. "*We* are. Right, *Mom*?"

Carla plays along. "We sure are, son of mine."

"Son of *yours*?" Mom is confused.

I gesture toward the crowd. "Wow, look at *all* the Z-Fans *everywhere*. Like, literally EVERYWHERE. I bet they'd freak if they saw the actual Z-Team. Like really,

really freak. If you know what I mean?"

Mom looks around at the herd of fans. "Oooooh, gotcha." She shakes Carla's hand. "Nice to meet you, *Mrs. Smith.*"

Chet plays along too, introducing himself to Dad, who's reduced to a speechless fanboy.

"Hey, look." Arturo elbows Chet. "You found the last Mantastic fan."

Destructo laughs. "I love this kid! Maybe I'll recruit him too. Speaking of recruits . . ."

"I like your hat."

Aaghh! Joy is hovering right next to my head! How long has she been there? Did she hear Destructo?

"Can I try it?" Joy reaches for my hat. . . .

"No!" I step back. "Get your own."

She grabs for it. "But I wanna try *yours.*"

I hold my hat tight against my head. "WELL. YOU. CAN'T. HAVE. IT."

She glares at me and clenches her tiny fists. That can't be good.

"Here ya go, princess." Chet steps between us, turning on the Mantastic charm. He holds out his hat. "You can have mine."

Joy's eyes narrow. "Stranger danger."

WHHHOOOOOOSH! A huge gust of wind blows Chet up and over Mega Mighty Mountain!

"Oh my!" Carla runs after him. "CHET! I mean . . . HUSBAND!"

Sweet! That's two down, eight to go. Things are looking up.

Till Joy makes her next move. "Mom?!"

"Your hat has been compromised," says Destructo. "It will self-destruct in twenty seconds."

Self-destruct?!

The *Jeopardy!* music plays as Destructo counts down. "Twenty, nineteen . . ."

"Mom?" Joy shouts again.

". . . eighteen, seventeen . . ."

I can't give my sister an exploding hat!

"Yeah, honey?" says Mom.

". . . sixteen, fifteen . . ."

"Can we go to VillainVille?"

Huh? Joy's giving up?

". . . fourteen . . ."

"Sure. Noah, you wanna come?"

". . . thirteen . . ."

"NO! I mean, no, thanks. We're gonna ride Mega Mighty Mountain."

". . . eleven, ten . . ."

Mom turns to Dad. "Do you think that's safe?"

Grandma pinches my cheek. "Yeah, maybe Mommy and Daddy can give baby Noah a stroller ride instead."

". . . seven, six . . ."

Destructo laughs. "Psych! Three, two . . ."

"What's *THAT*?" I point left, then chuck my hat right! It lands in a barrel of churros.

KABOOOOOOM!

Mom and Dad leap toward me but my friends are faster, surrounding me like a human super-shield as churros flop on the ground all around us.

"See?" I say to my cinnamon-and-sugar-dusted parents. "I'm totally safe."

Grandma shakes her head, "I don't know, cupcake, those churros were pretty scary."

Mom rolls her eyes. "Okay, fine. You know where we are."

As they walk away toward VillainVille, Joy shoots me a "you're welcome" look. I don't get it. Is she helping me? Don't know, don't care. That's four more down, and four to go. Now I just need to give my friends the slip.

Hugh chants through a mouthful of sidewalk churros, *"Mega Mighty Mountain! Mega Mighty Mountain!"* At least I think that's what he says.

I sit down on a park bench. "You guys go ahead. I'm gonna stay here and people-watch."

My friends stare at me blankly.

"People-watch? Seriously, dude?" Arturo asks in disgust.

"Yeah," I say, "I wanna take in the ambience."

"The *ambience*?" says Grandma as she waddles out of the crowd. "What are you, a grandma?!"

"Grandma?! I thought you—?"

"Puh-leeease! You think I'm gonna waste my day on kiddie rides?" She prods my friends with her walker. "Let's roll! I know how to disable the seatbelts on Mega Mighty Mountain."

They disappear into the crowd, leaving me gloriously alone.

I give it a few seconds until I'm sure the coast is clear, then hustle to the souvenir shop.

It's jam-packed with customers, but I spot the souvenir stones lining the back wall!

I squeeze through the crowded aisles, my eyes locked on the prize-perfect Super Stone replicas!

I reach for one, but stop short. I sense something . . . *creepy.* I turn as . . .

An entire shelf of Destructo toys rotate their evil little heads right at me!

CHAPTER 20

The Friend Lottery

Mission fail! Abort! Abort! I speed-walk out the exit and . . .

SMACK right into Ivy!

"Noah, what's going on?"

"Huh? What? Nothing. Just, uh . . . shopping."

"First people-watching, now shopping? Come on."

I hate lying. Especially to her. But I can't tell the truth, right? I mean, she's Ivy, but she's also super.

"You've been stressed all day. Yesterday too," Ivy says, searching my face. "You can trust me."

"It's just that you . . . well . . . you . . ."

"Have super-brain?"

Dang, she's good.

"Okay, sure," she says. "I have super-brain, but I also have *you*. You're my friend. That's more important to me than super-teams or powers or whatever. You know that, right?"

"Yeah. I know." Just saying it out loud feels like a thousand pounds lifting off my shoulders.

I pull Ivy around the corner, away from the crowd. Before I know it, I'm telling her everything. Her eyes get wider and wider until I finally run out of words.

There's a long, stunned silence as her eyes dart back and forth between mine.

"Soooo . . . *you*," she finally says, "all by yourself, with zero powers, have to double-cross our friends, the Five, Professor Möbius, and the world's number one super-villain. *Then* somehow hurl the Super Stone into the *SUN*?"

"Or . . . ," I say.

"Or we're all doomed."

"Exactly. You can see why I'm stressed."

"But, Noah, without the Super Stone, we'll . . ."

"You'll lose your powers. I know. And I'm sorry. But it's better than losing our world, right?"

Her face is still, and heavy. This is why I didn't want to say anything. The weight I felt is on her now. It makes my heart hurt.

Her eyes drift from mine. What's she thinking? Is she gonna hate me? I couldn't take that. Maybe I shouldn't have said anything? But it's all out there now. I just need to help her understand.

"Ivy," I say, "look around. What do you notice?"

"What? What do you mean?"

"Don't think about it. Just tell me what you see . . . what you hear . . . what you feel."

"Well . . . that old couple over there is sharing a Power Pretzel. . . . Those teenagers by the log ride . . . they're drenched, and laughing. . . . That bald man is really sunburned. . . . That lady's laugh is making her friends laugh. . . . And little kids on their parent's shoulders. . . . I smell popcorn, cotton candy, sunblock . . . and there's music, like old jazz, I think."

"Yep. What else? What's different than usual? What *don't* you see?"

She looks . . . searches. "Powers. Nobody's using their powers."

"Exactly. And it's pretty nice, right?"

She smiles, nods.

"Ivy, the world doesn't have to be super to be good. And I promise, I'm not jealous of everyone's powers. I mean, if the whole world loses their powers because of me, my life won't get better, it'll get worse. Everyone's gonna hate me forever. But they'll be safe. And they'll still have all of this."

A klutzy little girl twirls and bumps into Ivy as she dances to the park music.

Ivy laughs. She takes a deep breath. "Okay." She looks straight into my eyes. "What do we need to do?"

"We?" I ask.

"Yes, we. You aren't doing this alone. I'm gonna help you, every step of the way. So, what's first?"

Before I realize it, I'm bear-hugging Ivy and laughing like I won the friend lottery! So awkward, but so awesome.

Five minutes later, Ivy exits the souvenir shop and hands me a bag with a souvenir Super Stone. "Okay, now what?"

"Oh, no biggie," I say as I zip the souvenir stone inside my backpack. "I just need to learn how to fly a jet into outer space."

"No problem," she says.

"No problem? You know how to fly the Justice Jet?"

She grins. "Not yet."

"Huh?"

"Follow me!" She darts over to an information kiosk. Ivy scans a giant map of Power Park. "There!" Her finger lands on the Jammin' Justice Jet ride. "Let's go!"

Next thing I know, we're bouncing up, down, and side to side in the Justice Jet simulator! My lunch wants to make an appearance, but I hold it down and focus on the controls.

Which ones did Spider Monkey use? In what order? I twist a red knob. Nope! We slam against the wall. I pull a lever. Double nope! We nose-dive and the screen reads, "CRASH! Please exit the ride."

We unbuckle. I stumble out the door and dive into a trash can to deposit my lunch.

I stand up on wobbly legs. "Sorry about that."

Ivy puts her hand on my stomach. I feel a rush of healing as my nausea settles and blood returns to my head.

"All good?" she asks.

"Yeah, great. Thanks. Let's go again!"

We dizzily stumble out of the ride for the fifty-third time as the attractions shut down for the night.

Ivy zips up her jacket. "Well, we only crashed about twenty percent of the time toward the end."

"I'll take those odds," I say as I use my fingers to un-spin-cycle my knotted hair. "Well, I guess that's everything for today."

"Not everything," she says, taking my hand. "C'mon. We still have one more critical mission objective."

A few minutes later, Ivy walks out of the ice cream shop with two Super Sundaes. "I got triple-super scoops with quadruple fudge. You know"—she laughs—"in case this is our last meal."

We dig into our desserts as we slowly make our way down Mega Main Street toward the exit. I know tomorrow will be, well, terrifying. But that's tomorrow. Tonight . . . the lights, the music, the smell of warm cookies, tired parents carrying sleeping kids, a balloon stuck in a tree, quadruple fudge, Ivy smiling . . .

It's all perfect.

"Heeeeey, Dr. Brain-Man!" It's Tabitha, followed by Hugh, Arturo, and Grandma. They're all wearing Z-swag and glow-in-the-dark necklace things.

Tabitha is pumped. "Noah, Grandma's off her rocker! We gotta hang with her more."

"Yeah," Arturo mumbles through a mouthful of popcorn. "She got us to the front of every line!"

I laugh. "Grandma, heroes aren't supposed to cut in line."

"Who said anything about cutting?" Grandma shrugs. "Can I help it if people are afraid of giant snakes?"

We push through the turnstiles and head across the plaza to the Heroland Hotel.

We each have our own complimentary VIP suite but end up in Monkey's room instead. The rest of the night is a whole lot of laughing, pizza, and games.

It all feels so normal. Like the old days. I'll remember this night for the rest of my life.

Which is probably about six hours.

CHAPTER 21

One Bird, Two Stones

I slept about forty-two minutes last night, so the cool morning air blasting in my eyeballs is good medicine. I wonder if this is what coffee feels like.

Mantastic is giving me a lift, high above the park, en route to my mission starting position. Beneath us, Mega Main Street is overflowing with Z-Fans who camped out overnight to get the best seats for the parade.

"I underestimated you, little bro," Mantastic says as he sets me down on top of Mega Mighty Mountain. "You've turned out to be a straight-up solid hero."

Yeah, right. "I'm about to betray you along with the rest of the heroes" is what I'm *thinking*. What I actually say is "Thanks. You too."

"That means a lot. For serious." He holds out his fist for a bump. I bump it, and he flies off to take his position on the Power Dome.

I unzip my backpack. I've already checked it five times this morning, but one last time can't hurt. . . .

Souvenir Stone? *Check.*

Aluminum foil? *Check.*

Yep, it's all here—everything I need to pull off the biggest heist of all time!

Now I just need to . . . wait a minute, with all the chaos and crosstalk yesterday, I didn't hear how Magic plans to get me down to the Dome.

I scoot to the edge of the mountain. Below, the Z-Team parade is in full swing. Replay is shooting Candy Crush candies into the crowd. Hairstrike is giving hairy high fives, a dozen fans at a time. Hugh-Mongous is scooping up giddy kids and juggling them like bowling pins. Nightingale is flying back and forth, signing autographs and posing for selfies.

My family is in the VIP section. Mom and Dad are clapping along with the Z-Team music. Grandma's head is on top of a giraffe body—nobody's gonna block her view of the big event. As usual, Joy is in her own little weirdo world, scribbling in her notebook and ignoring everything hero-related.

Butterflies invade my stomach as the parade ends with a big, flashy dance number in front of the Power Dome. When did my friends learn to dance?!

«Ready, Noah?» It's Mindstorm over the mind link.

«Umm, I think so. . . . But just to be thorough, can you remind me what happens next?»

Unicorn Magic jumps on the link. «Hi, Noah! I've got you covered. It's just like we talked about yesterday!»

«Right, like we talked about, sure. But would you mind running through it just one more time?»

«Don't worry,» mind-says Magic. «You'll hate it, but it won't last long. Well, not too long anyway.»

«Wait, WHAT won't last long?»

«Just remember to keep your eyes open,» she says. «Closing them will only make it worse.»

«Only make WHAT worse?!»

«Oh, and breathe,» she adds. «That will help!»

«Breathe? Why wouldn't I BREATHE?!»

«Exactly, Noah! Okay, here we GOOOOO!»

Magical sparkles crawl up my legs and arms . . . chest . . . neck . . . face! My whole body tingles. What's happening?!

I BLAST OFF! *FZZZZZZZZ*, and streak through the sky, encased in a blazing cloud of rainbow dust!

"AAAAGGHHHHHHH!"

Oohs and aahs from the crowd drown out my horror screams. They can't see me. All they see is a Technicolor shooting star.

I swoop left, then right, forming a giant "S" in the sky! I nose-dive and loop back up, making a "U" shape. . . . Breathe. . . . Breathe. . . . Eyes open. . . . Open.

NOT HELPING! How long is this nightmare?!
Letter by letter, my rainbow contrail spells:

SUPERWORLD

The crowd goes wild!
Phew, it's over.
  Only it isn't! I loop and corkscrew on a never-ending torture coaster. . . .

SUPERWORLD CELEBRATES THE Z-TEAM! OUR NEW #1 HERO TEAM!

My rainbow comet plummets toward the Power Dome. It bursts into a million sparkly "Zs," showering the crowd with happiness and depositing me into a cramped hiding place behind the podium.

I catch my breath and force my eyes to focus . . . focus. . . . Möbius and the Five are right there, pretending not to see me.

Magic sneaks me a wink. «*Great job, Rocket Man.*»

The Dome Guards part, allowing the Z-Team to ascend and join us at the top.

The crowd hushes as my friends raise their right hands to take the Hero's Oath.

"We promise to defend Superworld, the Super Stone," *blah, blah, blah.*

The Five place medals around my friends' necks, declaring the Z-Team the WORLD'S #1 HERO TEAM!

The crowd roars!

Enormous holographic screens encircle the Power Dome. A multimedia show of the Z-Team's greatest moments shields us from the audience's view.

Game on!

I wriggle from my hiding place as Mantastic pulls the controller out from under his cape. He hands it to me, and I slip it into my backpack.

Everybody gathers around me with solemn "so proud of you" looks on their faces. I hope someday they'll understand I had no choice.

Ivy gives me a nod. At least she understands.

"Here ya go, Mission Possible." Spider Monkey clicks a harness with a cable around my chest.

"Look at him," Magic says. "Our hero. I wish I could swoosh you down, but our powers won't work in there until the Super Stone is safe and secure. After that, I'll twinkle you back up like a lightning bug!"

Möbius opens the secret hatch in the Dome.

"NOAH, ARE YOU READY TO SAVE THE WORLD?"

"Are you sure the Super Stone won't vaporize me?"

"I AM NINETY-EIGHT PERCENT SURE."

"Then I'm ninety-eight percent ready."

I hold my breath, as if that will help, and jump through the opening!

I plunge into darkness—

The cable snaps tight! Monkey lowers me down . . . down . . . down. . . .

Thud! I hit dusty ground.

My eyes adjust to the dim lighting and begin to focus. I'm sitting in a hole—a really wide, shallow hole—the *impact crater*. That means I'm inside the KILL RADIUS! I pat myself all over. Phew! Still solid.

Then it hits me: I'm all alone. Truly, utterly alone. No one can *hurt* me here. And no one can *help* me.

At the center of the crater, a blue-green sphere glows and shimmers—*the Super Stone*!

I stand up. Hold my breath. Then take a one-inch step toward it—no spontaneous combustion. I take a three-inch step. So far, so good!

The closer I get, the more nervous I feel. Am I a total idiot? Is this a terrible idea? I'm gonna be public enemy number one. Who am *I*, anyway? What am I even doing here?

I stumble over something. . . . What the . . . ?

It's a boot . . . a *pair of boots.*

Then all around me, I see capes, masks, and super-suits—all that's left of every hero and villain who tried to steal the Stone before me. I'm *standing in a graveyard!* I don't feel alone anymore, I feel surrounded. By empti-ness, and memory. All these people. . . . They used to be like me. They had families, friends, hopes, dreams. . . .

Then they became super, and nothing mattered . . . except *power.*

Enough! No more doubt! The Stone HAS TO GO!

I unhook my harness and hurry to the Stone.

Möbius was right, it's definitely cracked. Its power is leaking out like a toxic mist.

I haven't turned to dust, so I must be immune. But I'm still afraid to reach out and grab it. I mean, everyone in the world is afraid of this thing. Nobody has ever been this close. Nobody's ever touched it. Will it burn me? Or freeze me?

I hold my breath and slooooowly reach forward and . . . tap it with my finger, then yank my hand back! I check my finger. Looks normal. I exhale and breathe again. Okay, here goes.

I reach out and grab it!

Everything goes silent. The celebration outside fades away. I can barely hear my own breaths.

The Stone feels warm but not hot. It tingles on my skin, but it doesn't hurt. I lift it. . . . It's lighter than I expected.

It shimmers and shines, emitting its own light. It's beautiful. No, not really beautiful. But there's something about it. I want to look at it. I want to hold it. I don't know; it's strange. I want . . . *power.* I feel . . . empty . . . and *jealous.*

I shake my head. Whatever this thing is, I don't like it. Time to get back to work!

I carefully wrap it up in the very same foil that protected me from the Stone's power years ago. Once the foil is on, I feel more like myself. I can hear the muffled music and the cheering crowd again.

I gently place the Stone inside my backpack.

"NOAH?!" Rat's voice echoes and squeaks from the hatch high above. "You about done? The show's almost over!"

"Ummm, sort of! Working on it!"

"You're sort of working on it?!"

"Just give me a sec!"

I pull the souvenir stone from my backpack and snap it inside the controller. I spin the wheel, searching for the THUMBS-UP icon. Where is it? . . . Where is it . . . ?! Got it!

CLICK!

The controller screen lights up green. It reads:

SAFE

Okay. Almost done. Now I just have to wait for Destructo.

I look around, squinting and straining my eyes, trying to see into the darkness. Where is he? I don't really know what to expect. I mean I've only seen him in his mech-suit. But that thing would barely fit inside here.

"Hellooo?" I whisper.

«Noah? Noah, are you there?»

Oh no! It's Mindstorm! If I think anything, she'll know the Stone is neutralized, and Magic will zoom me back up!

Don't think, Noah. Don't think, don't think. . . .

«Noah, I'm sensing you. Do you have the Super Stone?»

Crud, where's Destructo?!

«Destructo? Did you say Destructo?»

Dang it! Stop thinking!

BOOOOOM! The Dome trembles and rings like a giant gong!

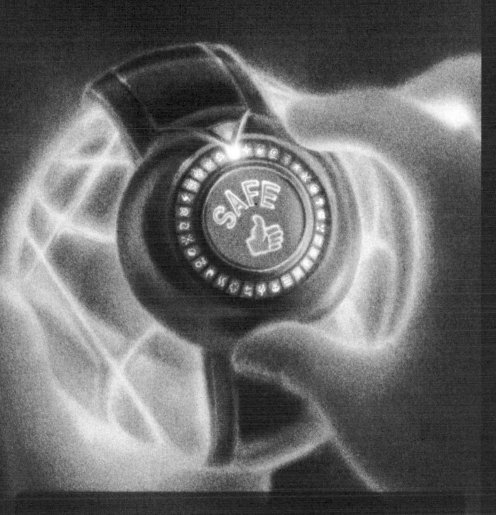

The mind link floods with panicked and confused thoughts. My friends are under attack!

Burning red light fills the Dome as a heat beam cuts a gigantic hole in the ceiling like an arc welder through butter! Then . . .

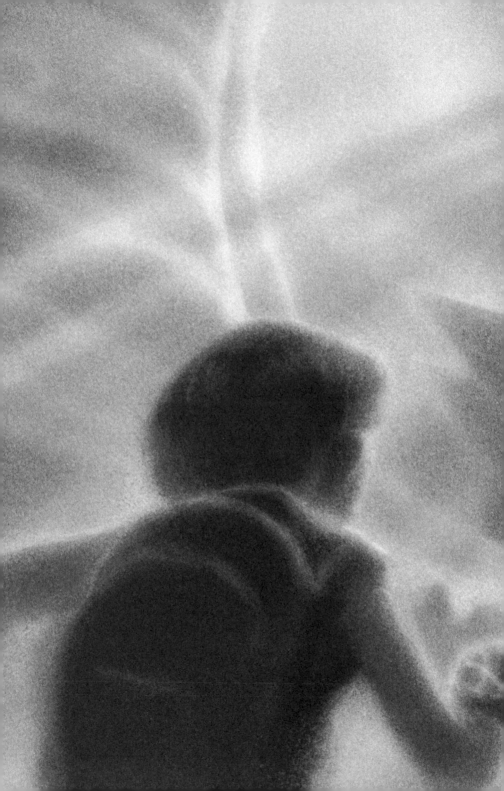

CHAPTER 22

The End of Superworld

"NOAH!" Dr. Destructo's eyes blaze red with rage. "You lying, cheating, double-crossing *villain*! What have you done?!"

The Dome amplifies his voice, rattling the ground around me.

"What do you mean? I . . . I . . . I . . ."

"YOU . . . YOU . . . YOU . . . *SAAAAVED THE WOOORLD*!" He breaks into his villain chuckle. "Ya done good, compadre!"

What's with this guy always trying to give me a heart attack?!

His giant claw reaches down. "THAAANK"– he plucks the controller from my hands–"YOU!"

He taps a button on his gigantic wrist. Villainous music plays, low and rhythmic– *BUM BUM BUM BUM–BUM BUM BUM BUM. . . .*

"Aaaaaall righty!" His foot thrusters ignite and lift him into the air. "It's showtime!"

He disappears in a column of fire and smoke as his villain music blends into the chaos outside.

Yup, it's showtime! Time to find Ivy and get to the Justice Jet before Destructo realizes his stone is fake!

I sprint to the opening in the wall. I leap and grab the edge. Owwwww! Still hot! Stupid heat beam! My hands sizzle like bacon, but I don't let go. I pull and wiggle, trying to swing my legs up. Dang, shoulda spent more time in PE!

Someone grabs my wrists. The burns on my hands cool from third degree, to second, to . . . It's IVY!

"Do you have the Stone?"

"It's in my backpack!"

Ivy lifts me out of the Dome . . . into a WAR ZONE!

The Z-Team and the Five are defending the Dome against hundreds of Destructo-Troopers! Everyone else in the park is losing their super-mind—switching into super-suits and brawling like it's their birthday.

Ivy flies us over the crowd, holding me like a football. We suddenly *drop*! She recovers. We climb up, up . . . then *drop again*!

"Ivy, are you okay?!"

"Yeah." She shakes her head. "Just dizzy."

She slings me over her shoulder like a sack of potatoes and zooms down Mega Main Street, dodging heroes, villains, beams, rays, bolts, and explosions.

Destructo music roars through every speaker in the park as he lands on the Dome behind us. He strikes a villain-victory pose as the musical score reaches a triumphant crescendo!

We're almost to the exit. . . . Almost to the Justice Jet . . .

We DROP, then skid, tumble, and SLAM into a popcorn stand!

"LET ME JUST START BY SAYING," Destructo's voice reverberates through the park, "YOU'RE WELCOME!"

Sweet, he's monologuing! This will buy us some time.

I dive behind the popcorn wreckage and do a quick status check—all 206 bones and the Super Stone . . . *still intact.* But where's Ivy?!

I scan the crowd. Everyone is frozen in mid-melee, transfixed by Destructo's villain speech. Everyone but my parents! Dad is flying over the crowd, scanning for me in every direction. Mom is XXXXL, frantically picking up rides and people like she's looking for car keys. Then I spot Ivy. . . .

She's behind me, across the street, struggling to stand.

I bolt toward her. "Ivy, what's wrong?!"

She winces with pain and falls to the ground. "I don't know. I feel—"

I stop and back away.

Her face relaxes. She takes a breath and stands, but she's swaying, holding her head.

"Ivy, I think . . . *it's the Stone*!"

"But you made it safe."

"I mean, I wrapped it in the foil. But it's not sealed. Its power must be getting through."

Destructo roars, "BEHOLD MY TRIUMPHANT AWE-SOMENESS, AND MARVEL AT YOUR GOOD FORTUNE AS YOU WITNESS"—the speakers screech with feed-back—"THE *DEATH OF SUPERWORLD*!"

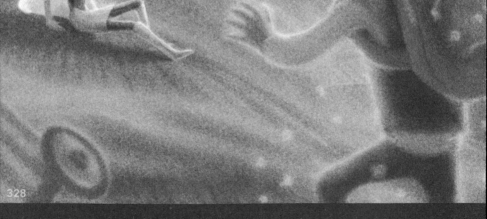

The crowd gasps!

"Noah." Ivy stumbles toward me. "We have to get out of here before he realizes . . ." She falls again.

"NO, Ivy!" I back up. "Stay where you are. It's too dangerous!"

"AND THE BIRTH OF . . . BUM-BA-DA-BUM-BUM-BUM," Destructo shouts in time with a long drumroll, *"DESTRUCTOOO WOOOORLD!"*

He raises the controller and fake stone above his head and lets loose a long, deafening laugh.

Every super-man, -woman, and -child races for the exit.

I shout over the stampede, "Ivy, I have to go NOW!"

"No! Not alone!"

BOOM! Mom's giant boot slams on the ground next to Ivy!

Mom kneels down. "Ivy, have you seen Noah?! I can't find him anywhere!"

Ivy stalls Mom. "Ummm . . . Noah . . . ?" then yells over Mindstorm's crowded mind link, «Noah, what do I do?!»

«You have to help me get away!»

«Noah, is that you?!» shouts Mindstorm. «Are you okay?! Destructo has the Stone!»

Crud, I keep forgetting she can hear our thoughts!

«Yeah, Mindstorm, uh . . . I'm . . . I'm fine. . . . Destructo . . . stole it from me.»

My friends and the Five flood the link with questions, «What's going on? Are you still in the Dome?! Noah, talk to us!»

I mind-shout, «IVY, PLEASE!»

"IVY, PLEASE!" Mom's voice is shaking. "I have to find him!" Mom sways, shrinks, rubs her head. The Stone is affecting her too!

«Don't worry, Ivy,» I say. «I can do this!»

Ivy tells Mom, "Um, Noah? He's hiding over there."

Ivy points toward Mega Mighty Mountain. Mom turns to look across the park, giving me my chance!

«Your chance? Your chance for what?» asks Magic.

Agh, stupid mind link! No more thinking, no more talking! I sprint for the exit!

Heroes and villains, weakened by the Stone, stumble and fall all around me. I bob and weave through them like a football player headed for the end zone.

I pop-vault and lemur-leap over the crowded exit structure, then under-bar, gecko-wall-run, and shoulder-roll out of the park!

I sprint to the Justice Jet, pop the hatch, and rush to the cockpit. I swing my backpack around to my front, then strap into the pilot's seat.

I scan the controls. *They're just like the simulator ride!*

I hit the ignition and slam the throttle!

The Justice Jet lurches forward, plowing through the parking lot, tossing cars, buses, super-mobiles. The wings catch a big gulp of air, and the jet leaps into the sky!

Moments later, I'm streaking over fields, then hills, then ocean.

Power Park is miles behind me now, but my mind is still crowded with my friends' voices. They're frantically calling for me over the mind link. My silence has thrown them into a panic; it's agonizing to hear. They think I'm hurt, or worse, but the mind link is fading . . . fading . . . gone.

I yank the wheel back, and the jet rockets upward. I scan the buttons. . . . *There!*

I punch the antimatter thrusters!

BOOOOM! I pancake deep into my seat as the jet jerks upward, shaking and shuddering as it rushes through the thick and roaring atmosphere.

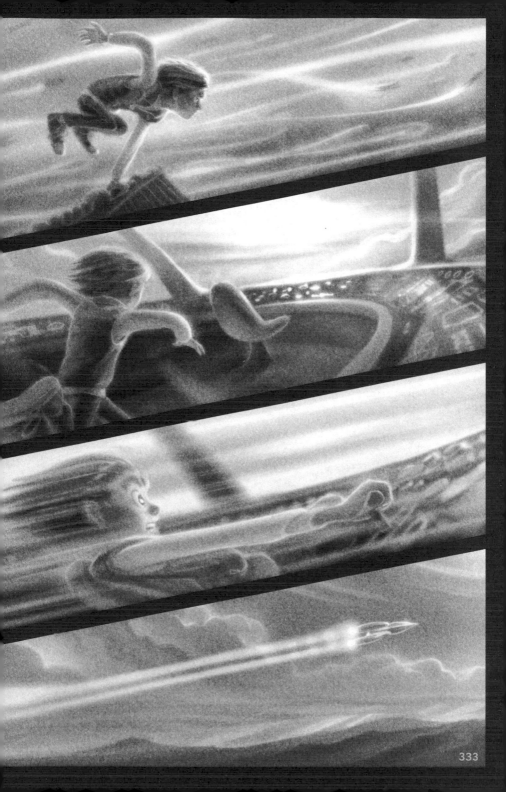

333

The blue sky gets deeper . . .

Darker . . .

Then black, speckled with a billion stars.

The shaking stops. The jet glides into the glassy smoothness of outer space.

I cut the engines.

My body unflattens and pops out of the seat. I'm weightless. Everything is still. Silent. Except for my breathing, and my mind.

I see the world below. . . .

So many battles flashing and smoldering like fireworks.

So much destruction.

For once, none of it can hurt me. I feel safe. Almost like I belong up here.

But everything and everyone I love is down there. It's my home. I *must* belong there.

I want to believe that.

I have to believe that.

It's the *Stone* that doesn't belong!

It stole *my world*.

I may never really get it back again, but I can save what's left for my family and friends. For all the heroes. Even for the villains.

Sunlight streams through the window. It tingles on my skin. The sun feels even more powerful out here. Okay, it's time to finish this!

I nudge the attitude thrusters until the sunlight streams directly through the airlock window.

I grab the seat and pull myself toward the airlock, drifting through the cabin. . . . *Flying*. . . . So this is what it feels like.

I unzip my pack and gently pull out the foil-covered Super Stone.

I open the airlock's inner door and place the Stone inside, leaving it floating in midair.

I close the door, then "fly" back to the cockpit.

My finger hovers over the button for the outer hatch. "Enjoy your nonstop flight to annihilation."

I punch the button.

The hatch flies open. Air rushes into the vacuum of space, launching the Super Stone toward the sun!

I watch until the sunlight stings my eyes. I look away, squinting and blinking. As my eyes recover, I see . . .

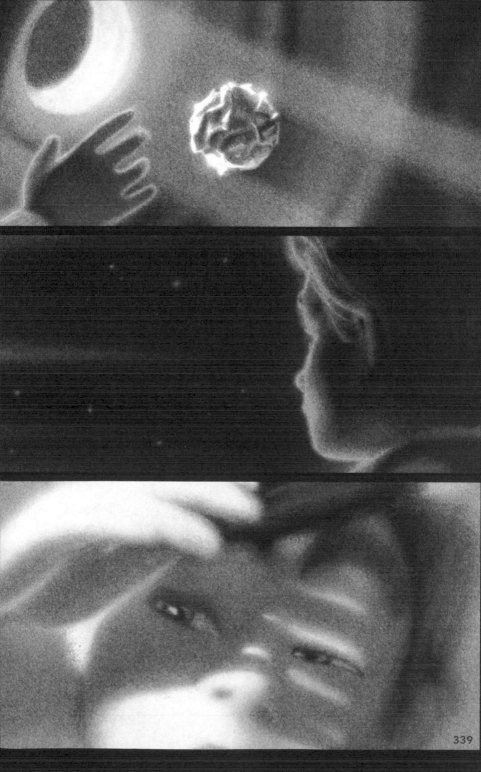

The Earth. My home.

It's safe now.

I did it.

I actually did it!

The whole world is gonna hate me.

But Mom and Dad will love me no matter what.

And Ivy understands. Hopefully the rest of my friends will too.

Someday.

Whatever happens next, it'll be okay.

I did what I could to protect them. To protect everyone.

I think that was my purpose.

My skin suddenly cools.

Darkness crawls across the cockpit.

A shadow?

I turn. . . .

The sun is eclipsed by . . .

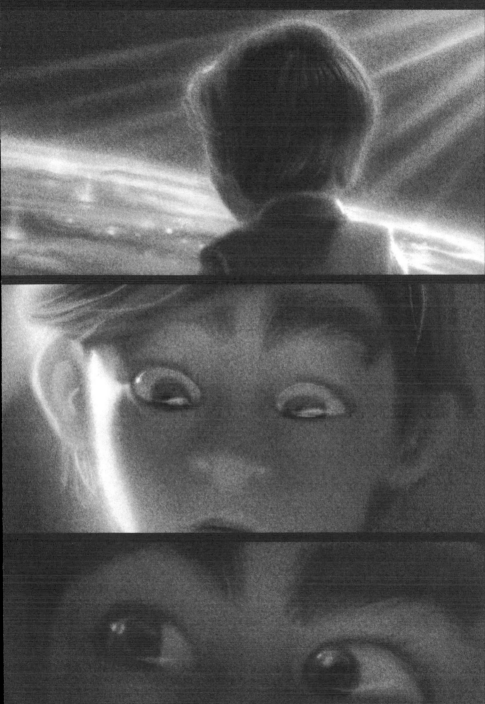

Dr. Destructo!

Music booms through the jet's speakers—

DUN-DUN-DUUUUUUNN!

CHAPTER 23

Know Your Enemy

Destructo's theme music swells and builds to a frenzy, sending a thumping wave of triumph through the ship's hull--rattling the air, my chest, my teeth.

"Aluminum foil?!" His voice buzzes over the fading reverberations of his musical punch in the face. "You've gotta be kiddin' me. This whole time I coulda wrapped the Stone in foil?!"

What's going on?! How did he--?!

The mech's head jerks back. "Whoa . . . not really a tight seal, is it?" He stretches out his arm, keeping the Stone as far away from his head as possible. "Makin' me a little woozy. Maybe use some tape or glue next time."

He raises his other claw. *It's holding the controller!*

"Ha! Kidding! Like there's gonna be a next time."

Destructo snaps the Super Stone into the controller and, *boop,* clicks the dial to SAFE. "Aaaaaah, that's better."

He flicks the foil away from the blazing Stone. "Seriously, how did you figure out the foil thing? Do you know how long it took me to invent this controller?"

Huh? What's he talking about? He didn't invent the controller--*Möbius did.*

Destructo's monstrous mech-head leans in close. His gigantic eyes flood the cockpit with blazing red light. Someone is standing behind one of the eyes, just beyond the glass . . . a man . . . wearing *little round sunglasses.*

What?! Dr. Destructo is . . .

345

PROFESSOR MÖBIUS!

He waves. "SURPRIIIIIISE!"

"I don't . . . ?! How . . . ?!"

"HA! Gotcha! *Gotcha, gotcha, gotcha!*"

My head is pounding. Cold sweat is running down my face.

"Come on, Noah, it's your turn to say something. This is when you're like, 'Noooooooooooo! This can't beeeeeeee! I've been outsmarted! Outwitted! Out-bamboozled!'"

My mind is in full system overload, processing it all, putting pieces together.

"This is the best part, kiddo! Well, for *me* anyway. This is when you realize I've been one step ahead of you the whole time." Destructo leans back in a long fit of irritating villain laughter.

My chest feels tight . . . empty. What have I done? I let him win. I *helped* him win!

I want out . . . to shut down. Give up. Fade away. . . .

NO! Don't give in! DO . . . something!

I hook my foot under the pilot's seat and slyly pull myself toward the controls as he locks eyes on me again.

"That's right, Noah! I've been with you all along. Do you know what a Möbius strip is? It's an object that seems to have *TWO sides* . . . but really has *ONE!*"

I glance down at the controls, then back at him. In that split second, I spot the ignition, the throttle. . . .

"There is no Professor Floaty-Head. There is only Dr. Destructo—the most brilliant, evil genius the universe has ever known!"

I slam the ignition and yank the throttle hard into REVERSE! The jet blazes to life!

Destructo casually taps a button on his gauntlet. The jet's systems groan . . . whir . . . and power down.

"Never interrupt a villain's gotcha speech, Noah. It's bad form."

I slam and pull every button and lever. . . . Nothing. The jet is dead!

"I have to admit, buddy, you made this whole thing a lot more fun! I had a simple, boring plan: *Make the Muscleheads number one by eliminating the Five. Have you steal the Super Stone and give it to Möbius. Blow everybody's minds when I reveal Möbius is really me.*

Then rule the world. Easy-peasy! But then you went rogue! You switched your team and saved the Five. That was *very* unexpected."

I think as hard as I can, trying to reach the mind link. «*MINDSTORM?...IVY?...MANTASTIC?...MAGIC?...*»

No one's there.

"I needed to break up your little hero party, so I hatched a new plan: *Make you doubt the heroes and your friends so you'd double-cross them and give the Stone to me instead.* But then you figured out your little tinfoil trick and double-crossed me too. *ME!* Not cool, Noah. NOT COOL. You just made me look like an idiot in front of all my fans and fanemies!"

"You thought you'd beaten me, but you were wrong! That's my jet you stole, rookie. Ever heard of GPS? All I had to do was follow you up here."

The air in the cockpit is thinning. . . . My brain . . . getting dizzy . . .

"Believe it or not, home fry, this is a sweet-and-sour moment for me. After shadowing you all these years, I've grown kind of fond of you. I mean, you seem pretty cool. Your family likes you; you're a good friend. . . . I thought maybe we'd be friends someday too. I actually thought it was *meant to be.*

"Ya see, back when the Stone hit, I knew it would be mine someday. I just didn't know how. Then I saw you splattered across the evening news. That's when everything clicked into place! I knew you and I were cosmically linked—like mac and cheese. I knew *my* purpose, and I knew *yours*!"

His words swirl in my . . . foggy . . . mind. . . .

The glowing insignia on his chest irises open, revealing a hollow chamber. "In that moment, I knew *YOUR destiny* was to fulfill *MY destiny!* I'm so glad you're here to see it all come together. To see your purpose fulfilled. To see *this* . . ."

He holds the controller and the Stone out in front of his mech. "Ready, partner?"

He lets go. It streaks into his chest like a magnet and clicks into place.

A blaze of power rushes from the Stone into the suit. The space around him is thick with energy that shudders the jet, rippling through it. . . .

"WOOOO! This feels GOOOOOOOOD!"

His enormous claw reaches out and grabs the jet. "Well, amigo, it's been fun! But all good things must come to a fiery end . . . *for you, anyway.*"

He cocks his arm back like he's holding
a paper airplane.

"Now sit back, relax, and enjoy your
nonstop flight to annihilation."

He hurls the jet toward the sun. "Wheeeeeeee!"

I'm thrust back against the seat!

White-hot sunlight scorches my eyes.

I gasp . . . for air.

There's . . . none . . . left. . . .

I'm . . . alone.

Everything . . . goes . . .

EPILOGUE

Thirty minutes earlier . . .

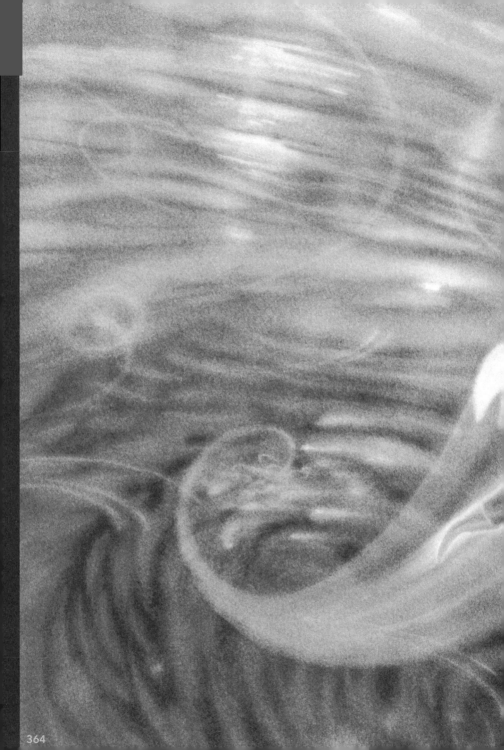

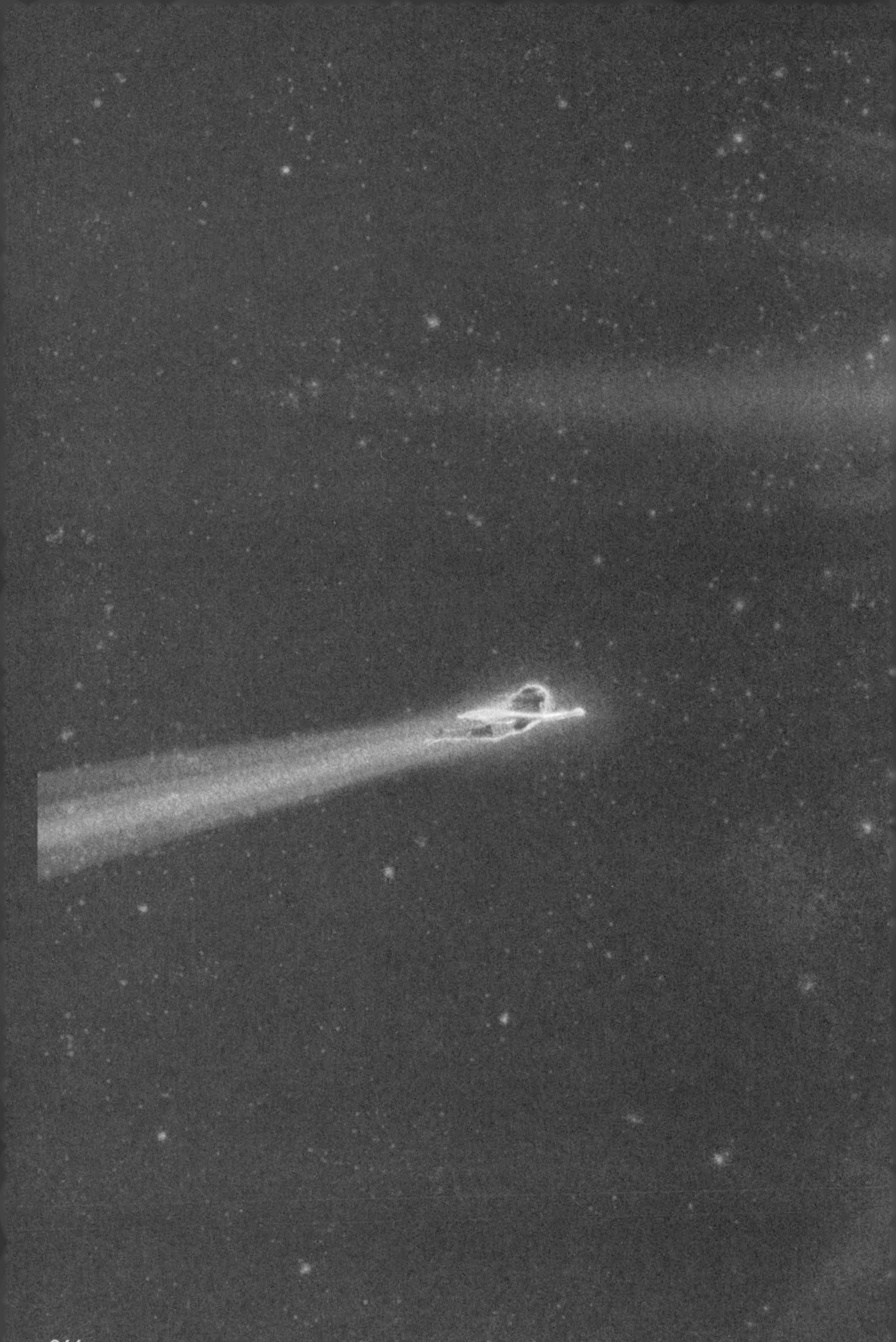

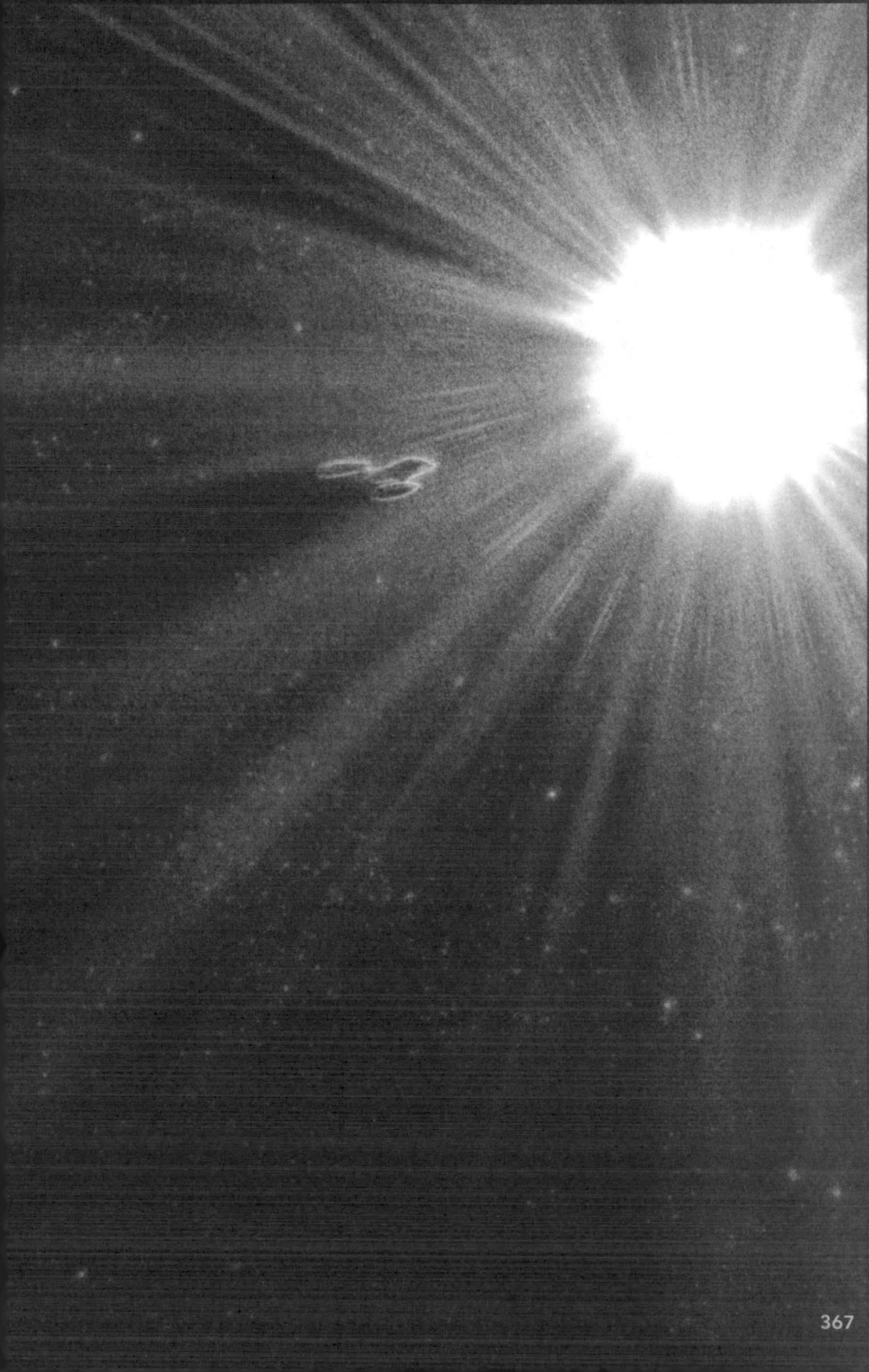

To be continued . . .

WELCOME TO DESTRUCTO WORLD
PEACE THROUGH WORLD DOMINATION
You're Welcome!
Don't miss
~~SUPERWORLD II~~
DESTRUCTO WORLD
Coming very, very soon! (But not soon enough!)

Acknowledgments

A super-mega-mighty-power THANK-YOU to . . .

Michelle Nagler, for being wonderful from minute one. We're so grateful for your shepherding and encouragement. We couldn't have dreamt of having a more creative and supportive editor. Thanks for taking a chance on a couple of rookies!

Jasmine Hodge, Barbara Bakowski, Alison Kolani, and Rebecca Vitkus for your editorial superpowers.

Bob Bianchini, for your expertise and help in getting this Hugh-Mongous-sized project across the finish line.

Andrew Cannava, for all you've done to make this new chapter in our lives possible.

Albert Lee, for your coaching, support, and contagious enthusiasm!

Mary Pender, for your invaluable guidance and input from so early on.

Nancy Newhouse Porter, for your friendship and great care over all these years.

THANKS, one and all. We're beyond blessed to have such an amazing super-team!